MAJKA

by A. L. SYLVESTER

RoseDog Books
PITTSBURGH, PENNSYLVANIA 15238

RoseDog Books
585 Alpha Drive, Suite 103
Pittsburgh, PA 15238
Visit our website at *www.rosedogbookstore.com*

ISBN: 978-1-4809-8189-8
eISBN: 978-1-4809-8212-3

I want to dedicate this book to my family; but especially to my daughters who were an unfailing source of encouragement, I wrote this as a Christmas gift for them and they encouraged me to share my work.

All names and places in this book do not refer to actual persons living or dead.

Thank you

Prologue

The clock struck the witching hour of three A.M. The dark lake shimmered with the reflection of the full moon. The wind started to gust, slowly picking up speed to gale force. The trees bent over and the leaves scattered in a circular motion. Clouds began to move in slowly, covering the moonlight. Thunder rumbled in the distance.

Two elderly sisters sat side by side in rocking chairs looking out at the scene developing before them. They both had white hair in braids. One wore her braid straight down her back; the other to the side. Their skin was worn, wrinkled and thin as tracing paper.

"It is almost time." The younger said to her sister.

"Do you think they will like it?" The older sister replied.

"I don't know." The first one replied very seriously, looking straight outside. "They will have to work together."

"I hope they do." The second one said with a sad sigh turning back to the black shining lake.

"They have no choice," was the reply as the first bolt of lightning struck the lake as a clap of thunder shook the house. They both sat quietly, petting the white lynx cats on their laps. They reached out and clasped hands and they closed their eyes.

To the cats they said, "Take care of them."

Chapter 1

It was early morning, mid-September, with an overcast sky and a nip in the air. Steph woke up with the phone ringing. She pulled the blankets up over her head, snuggling further under her blankets, trying to ignore the nagging sound. She contemplated letting it go to voicemail, but she knew her mailbox was full, as usual. She gave in, rolled over, grabbed her cell phone off the side table and pulled it back under the covers with her. With a groggy voice she answered the phone. "Hello, yes, this is Stephanie, what do you mean my grandmother in Maine?" She sat up in bed. "My mother said she died before I was born!! No! I cannot ask her!" She got all choked up, her mom had died just a few months ago and who was this moron asking her about it? She felt her heart rip in half as it always did when she thought of her mom. She had been on her own, in a small apartment in New Hampshire. She took a deep breath and held back her tears. "Fine, I will be there. I am just going to sell it. It is a waste of time for me just to go all the way up there. Can you email or fax me the documents? Fine." The strawberry blond ended the call on her cell phone. Wearing a large oversized flannel shirt as pajamas, she slowly got out of bed, padded her way down the hall to her small kitchen, and started a pot of coffee, turning up the heat as she passed the thermostat. While she waited for the coffee, she paced around her apartment that she adored so much. She loved the light green walls and the old worn furniture. She plopped herself down on the small love seat and tucked her feet up under her. She was frustrated by this phone call and completely confused. She picked up the book she had set down before going to bed. She couldn't even read one sentence; she had so many questions running through her head. It is going to mess up all her routine.

At the age of eighteen Stephanie was very responsible. Her mother always called her an "old soul." Running her hands through her hair she stood up and sighed, she made a phone call to start arranging her leave of absence from work. All she wanted was one day to sleep in and today was her day off. Now she had so much to do. She would be leaving in a week. She looked around her small apartment wondering what to pack and how much she would need. She kept thinking of her mom and how she could have told her about her grandmother. She had no idea that she had a grandmother who was alive or was recently alive, and what was she going to do with a house that she co-owned with a cousin she didn't know she had? And why had her mother never mentioned any family? She stopped pacing in front of the mirror and took a long look at herself. She was short and petite. She had curly strawberry blond hair and bright blue eyes that people say glowed when she got upset.

• • • • •

Later that afternoon, a few hundred miles from New Hampshiret, a pretty dark- haired girl danced around her living room with the music blasting. The base of the music radiated throughout the walls. She picked up her clothes off the floor while dancing. When she felt her cell phone vibrate in her pocket, she picked up the remote and turned the music down and answered her phone. "Hello," she said out of breath. "Yes, this is Sayer, your name is... Newt? OK. Really? You're kidding me, Sure I can go! I have nothing here holding me back. I will see you then." "Wow," she thought. I have a house! My luck has turned. Time to ditch this dingy studio apartment. She was surprised to find out that she had a grandmother or that she had a family! This meant that she didn't have to grow up in a foster home. If she had known her grandmother was alive all this time and was going to leave her a house, her life would have been so much different. Why had she not known this? She could not help but feel kind of pissed off, but still happy that her newly discovered grandmother had left her half a house. To her cat she said, "Time for us to move on, again."

• • • • •

Sayer lived in an apartment above a garage. It was small, and the heat worked most of the time and the AC worked only in the winter. The landlord ignored her complaints, but Sayer was able to have a garden in the backyard, so she just kept her mouth shut and dealt with it. She looked around her small apartment. She had futon on the far wall that was her bed and also served as her couch when people come over, which was hardly ever. To the left was a small kitchenette if you could even call it a kitchenette. It consisted of a microwave, toaster oven, coffee pot and a sink. She was an expert with cooking on such basic appliances. On the back wall was a large window looking over the back yard. She had a small table in front on the window that she had picked it up from the side of the road. Someone had put it out for trash. She though one man's trash is one girls table, and she had two matching chairs that she picked up at Goodwill.

"You know, Charlie, I am not going to miss this place at all," she said to her cat who was napping in the sun on the futon.

Chapter 2

Less than a week later, Sayer was standing outside the Portland Airport looking for her ride. The wind was blowing so hard that she pulled her dark hair into a ponytail and zipped up her North Face. She was so excited. The sky was bright blue, and the leaves were just starting to turn. Fall had come early in Maine. The sound of jet planes taking off and landing filled the background. She had one duffel bag of clothes and a cat carrier with her orange cat "Charlie" in it. Saying to the cat, "We are going to be fine; fuzz ball; Living in Maine is going to be great! I can feel it."

A blue BMW pulled up and the passenger side window went down. Sayer looked in to see a kindly looking gentleman with glasses, dark hair and a goatee that was just starting to gray, and he asked, "Are you Sayer O'Brian?"

"It depends, are you Newton Curtis?" Sayer asked.

"Yes, I am attorney at law Newton Curtis at your service." He got out of the car and pulled out his ID to show her. "But just call me Newt. I am sorry for your loss," he said while taking her bags. "Is this all you have?" He asked, gesturing to the duffel bag and the carrier. "Yup, I figured since I was getting a house I didn't need my old furniture, so I sold it to my landlord. He took it and said it would count for my last month's rent so it all worked out, and thank you for your kind words, but, to be honest, I never met the lady. I was told she had died before I was born," she said all in one nervous breath.

"It must have come quite of a shock to find out that you had a grandmother and a cousin you didn't know about?" Newt inquired as he was putting her bag in the trunk of his car.

"Tell me about it. Not only that, but I own a house with her," Sayer bubbled.

"Your cousin wants to sell the place," Newt informed her.

"I will buy her out, once I get a job and enough money," Sayer replied with a smile as she opened the back door of the car. Looking inside at the plush interior and could imagine the damage the car carrier will do. She looked at Newt and asked "Um, do you happen to have a towel to put under Charlie's cage?"

"No, but don't worry about it. It is leather and can take it." Newt replied with a wink and continued, as they got in the luxurious car. "It is stated in the will that it goes to each of you and you have to live together." Newt said looking at her over the top of his glasses.

"I will just have to change her mind then," Sayer said with excitement in her voice as she looked around the car. She thought it was the fanciest car she had ever been in. "Wow, this is so nice," Sayer said as she ran her hands over the leather seat.

Smiling Newt replied 'Thank you. You have accepted this situation surprisingly well" Newt stated as he pulled out into traffic. He took the northbound ramp onto Interstate 95. They zoomed up the highway and the further they went the less they saw of civilization. In not time all, they were passing nothing but tall trees. Sayer relaxed and was enjoyed the scenery. She picked up the conversation. "Like I said on the phone, I had nothing holding me back. I had a dead-end job, a crappie apartment, and no boyfriend. The only person or animal I can count on is myself and Charlie here. It has been just the two of us for a long time now," Sayer said as the cat gave a soft "meow," looking insulted for being in a cage.

"How did you get the name Sayer? It is very different," Newt asked.

"I don't know but I bet my mom could not spell and screwed up the birth certificate," Sayer said with a shrug. "But I like it, no one else has it," she smiled at Newt with her eyes twinkling.

During the forty-five-minute drive up the Maine Interstate she learned Newts background. She found out that Newt had put in four years in the Navy, went to law school and now is the local attorney. He had taken over his father's firm. His law practice is small enough that he could take care of the local families with the drawing up of wills, real-estate documents, and the occasional divorce. He found that he could do it part time, leave the big stuff for the younger, more ambitious lawyers in the big city and enjoy his semi-retirement of cooking, performing in the local theater group, and fishing. He lived in a small house just up the road from her grandmother's place, which is just a short mile from her new home.

Sayer found Newt to be charming and easy to talk to. He was like a young grandfather with a quick smile, a glint in his eye and a corny sense of humor. She instantly liked him.

They pulled into a bumpy road and traveled about quarter mile and then the trees opened to show a large house that must have looked majestic in its time. "Oh my, I love it," Sayer exclaimed. "It is nothing like I imagined!" The house was a large brick New Englander style house, with ivy growing all over it. The flower beds were overgrown, and the grass looked like a field of hay. "I can get those flower beds back in order in no time and I love the ivy, it just needs to be trimmed back some. I have sort of a green thumb," she said with pride in her voice looking over at Newt.

Newt chuckled to himself. "Then you are in for a big surprise."

Sayer got out of the car and grabbed Charlie from the backseat. Newton pulled out a key and gave it to Sayer. "It is your place now." They walked up the stone steps. Sayer unlocked the door gave it a push and nothing happened. She turned to Newt with a quizzical expression. "It sticks sometimes, push harder" he said encouraging her. She did, and the door slowly opened to reveal a wood paneled entry. She took a step inside and let out the breath she was holding. Sayer put down the cat carrier to let out the feline. He didn't run out. He just sat there with his tail twitching. "Do you smell a mouse already Charlie?" Looking back at Newt she said, "I will just leave him and when he is ready he will come out." She felt overwhelmed.

There was a door to the left and one to the right. Sayer chose the right-hand door first. She opened the door and stepped into a large dining room. It had a long cherry table with matching hutch. The hutch was filled old antique china. Everything had a layer of dust on it. The walls were a faded tan color. It had crown molding around the ceiling. There was a fireplace in the back-left corner and large windows in the front of the house covered by thick flowered drapes. In the back-right corner was another door. Sayer opened the door to a country style kitchen and just stood in shock. She could see all the way at the other end of the kitchen to a room just overgrown with lush plants. She walked with an open mouth past a butcher block stand, past an old cast iron stove, and a porcelain country style sink. She opened the door to a solarium with more plants than she had ever seen. She turned to Newt and said," I love it."

He laughed and said, "You haven't seen the rest."

"I don't care. I am never leaving." She couldn't stop smiling. She opened the door to the solarium and stepped inside. Sayer inhaled the smell of damp earth and plants. It was warm and moist. She looked at all the plants. Some she recognized, and a lot she did not. "Do you know what all these plants are?" she asked Newt. "No, but you can figure it out; I am sure. Let me show you the rest of the house," he replied. Reluctantly Sayer followed him, and they continued with the tour. From the left of the solarium they walked into a very cozy living room with double doors that opened to a wrap-around deck. The couch and loveseat in the living room were worn and mismatched but in somehow looked good together. They were big and inviting, if you sat in one you would just sink in and never want to get up. The walls were a soft shade of green. This room also had a fireplace. Sayer noticed that there was no TV. "Newt, where is the TV?"

"Your grandmother did not watch TV."

"Oh," she sadly said. Her TV was one of the items she sold to her landlord. "What happened to her, my grandmother? Why did she leave me a house? Why didn't she ever contact me?" Sayer asked.

"Well to be honest, no one knows. Your grandmother Emma lived here all her life with her sister Sophie. No one had seen them in a year. They just disappeared. An investigation turned up nothing but a will that was locked in the library. That is how I found you. She had your address tucked in with the will. I wish I had more answers for your questions why she never came looking for you. If it wasn't for her will, I would not have known how to find you.

“That is creepy. What was she like besides a stalker? If she knew where to find me all this time why did she leave me in foster homes?” Sayer asked.

“Sayer, I have to say that you look so much like Emma, the same dark hair and the piercing blue eyes but I don’t know what to tell you. I don’t have any answers for you.” Newt said sadly to her. “But she was a wonderful person. Loved her books and was very serious and level headed. Her sister Sophie was always tinkering with stuff. Like that plant room. It has an automatic watering system. She hooked up a pump that pulls from the well under the house. That is why the plants are still alive. Sophie loved to dance and didn’t have a care in the world. She always said things have a way of working themselves out. Whereas, your grandmother like to plan everything out. Detail by detail.”

“It sounds like I have more in common with Sophie than my grandmother.” They continued around to the front of the house on the opposite side of the dining room. There was the said library with lots of old books and a huge mahogany desk. “I have no use of this room. I hate to read.”

“Emma, your grandmother loved this room, but her sister Sophie didn’t care for it.” Newt said.

Sayer felt like someone was watching her. She turned around and saw her cat but didn’t think that was it. “What do you think Charlie?” The fat cat just looked at her, put his ears back and walked off, jumped up onto the loveseat and curled up to take a nap like he had lived there all his life. Sayer just shook her head. She looked at Newt and asked, “I wonder what Stephanie is like?”

“You will know soon enough. She will be here tomorrow.”

Newt left Sayer to get herself settled. She walked around the first floor one more time. This did not feel real, like she was in a dream and she was afraid she would wake up and it would be over. Taking a deep breath, she took her bag and headed up the stairs to check out the rooms upstairs. There were four bedrooms. It had two bedrooms on the front of the house and two on the back. There was a bathroom on each side separating the two rooms. The back rooms each looked over the driveway. The two rooms on the front side each had large French doors that opened to a deck overlooking the lake. Each bedroom was furnished with large queen size beds and dark Victorian furniture. Sayer chose the room done in light yellow overlooking the lake. She walked to the doors that lead to the deck, opened them, and walked out; she took a deep breath, and just enjoyed the peaceful view of the lake. There was a light breeze and the air was crisp. She left the door to the deck open to air out the room because the room had a musty, closed -up smell. She walked back inside and lay down on the large bed on her back. Charlie jumped up and joined her on the bed. “What do you think?” she asked him. “Do you like it?” Charlie started purring and curled up in a ball and went to sleep. She figured she got her answer. Sayer got up and started to open and close the drawers in the dresser. They were full of clothes who she assumed belonged to either Sophia or Emma. She went to what she guessed was the closet and was pleased to see that it was deep. Not a walk -in closet, but deep enough that you could store things in the back easily. She went into the bathroom attached to the room. The closet had towels and was well stocked with all the basics. She smelled the shampoo. It was grape scented. She opened the door opposite of the one she had walked through, and it took her to one of the rooms overlooking the street. This room was painted a pale blue. She checked the closet and drawers in the room and found them to be empty. She continued to the room across the hall. This room was a light pink and she found it empty too. She entered the other bathroom. Sayer found it to be the same as the first one but with different supplies, then she went through the door into the other bedroom overlooking the lake. This one was decorated in a pale green. She found the closet and drawers full too. She made a mental note to pick up some boxes to pack away the stuff and some trash bags to clean out the bathrooms. She figured she should wait until Steph got there and they could do it together. After all, as cousins they should share the decisions about their grandmothers’ things.

Sayer spent the rest of the day poking around the first floor. She opened more windows to air the first floor out. She took a long look at the cast iron stove. It was beautiful with all the art work put into the castings. She thought it should be in a museum and then was relieved to see that it has been converted to gas at some point. She got a mental image of herself filling it full of wood and going through a pack of matches just to cook some eggs. With a small giggle, she shook the image out of her head. She figured a good way to get to know the place was to clean it up so; she started to dust the first floor and wipe down the counters. She went through all the drawers and the cabinets in the kitchen to see what she had to work with and started a list of supplies she felt that she needed. She spent a lot of time in the solarium checking out the plants. There were a lot she had never seen before.

In the late afternoon, she started to clean the room she planned to use. She found clean sheets in the linen closet in the hallway. She made up her bed and decided to settle down for the night. It had been a long day and tomorrow was going to be one too. She was looking forward to meeting Stephanie. What would she be like? Would she be outgoing or shy? Short or tall? Happily thinking she was going to finally have a family. She opened the door to the deck all the way to let the breeze off the lake in and crawled into bed. She was exhausted. As she was falling asleep she was still thinking about meeting Stephanie, and in her half-conscious mind she thought she heard voices but figured it was just the wind in a strange house. She slept soundly and completely that night.

Chapter 3

The sun was just cresting the horizon as Steph got ready to hit the road. She had a "to-do" list in her hand and checked off things for the third or fourth time. She was very meticulous and detailed orientated. She had a part time job at an insurance company while in high school and when she graduated she was offered a full-time position. When her mom passed away she was able to keep the small apartment that they had shared. She loved it there. Stephanie and her mom had acquired all the furniture together from used furniture stores and had refurbished the pieces themselves. They had an old couch of blue, a recliner that was done in a plaid pattern and a small TV. One wall was covered by a built-in book shelf. It was crammed full of books. They both had loved to read. They would spend quiet evening reading and drinking tea. Her mother had kept telling her she needed to get out and enjoy her youth, but Steph always told her there will be time for that when she was well again.

• • • • •

Now all she had to do was go to Maine and unload the house and get back to her home. Her small Toyota was packed. She has her toll money ready and a full tank of gas. I guess there is nothing left to do but get it over with, she thought, as she put on an audio book and started out for Maine.

• • • • •

Two and a half hours later Steph was on the side of the road looking at a map. She had put the address in her GPS on her phone, but it hadn't found the address. She had to backtrack a mile or two and take a dirt road on the right. It was a long bumpy road that opened to a house that looked rundown and overgrown. She let out a sigh thinking that it will need some work to get the most market value. She parked that car in the driveway and walked up to the door.

• • • • •

Steph knocked on the door with an old brass knocker that had turned green. She wiped her hands on her jeans and she heard feet skipping to the door. The door flew open and she stood there looking at a mirror image of herself except for the hair. The girl who opened the door had dark hair and no freckles. Steph and Sayer just stood and stared at each other. The two girls said at the same time "Oh My God." They felt a light breeze pass from inside the house like a contented sigh, like the house had been holding its breath and could finial let it out. "Did you feel that?" Steph asked Sayer.

"Yes, but this is an old drafty house. There are fireplaces in almost all the rooms. You must be Steph," Sayer said. Sticking out her hand.

"Yes, and you must be Sayer," Steph said. Taking her hand and shaking it.

"Come into your new home, you are going to love it, it is amazing!" Sayer replied and stepped aside to let Steph in.

"I just want to get back home. Would you be interested in buying my half?" Steph said while stepping through the door and looking at the dark paneled room, hoping that the rest of the house was not so out dated.

"I would love to, but Newt said we both have to live here. It is in the will," Sayer said.

"Who is Newt?" Steph asked

"He is the lawyer who called us. He was our grandmother's lawyer. He is very nice. He lives about a mile down the road. I will call him, so you can meet him, and he can explain everything. He half-filled me in a bit but wanted to wait until we are both together for the rest," Sayer said.

"Oh, that's right. Let's get this over with," Steph replied.

" I will show you around," Sayer said taking a sideway glance at Steph.

"What is in the cabinets" Steph asked gesturing to the back of the foyer?

"I have no idea. I hadn't noticed them" Sayer said as she walked over and pulled on one of the doors. It did not open. She pulled harder, nothing. It must be stuck. Sayer suggested they come back to it later.

Sayer knew she had to find a way to make her cousin love the place as much as she did. Sayer started the tour of the house. She brought her into to the dining room first. "This is some nice furniture," Steph said in awe looking at the old Victorian set. She walked over to the hutch and peered inside. She opened the door and pulled out a plate. She flipped it over and looked at Sayer with surprise. "Did you know that this china is from the 1600s?"

"No," Sayer said just looking at Steph. She didn't know what to think. As far as she was concerned, it was just old china.

"This may be worth some money?" Steph said. Sayer looked at her like she had three heads.

"Is this place full of antiques like this? I had no idea. I had pictured old worn out stuff smelling like mothballs," Steph said with a smile. "Let's see the rest of the place." Her whole demeanor seemed to lift a little as they went through and into the kitchen.

Steph walked over to the cast iron stove. "Will you look at this? It's awesome. The detail in the cast iron is so cool." She ran her hand over the stove and felt all the details in the castings. This gave Sayer some hope that maybe she could change Steph's mind. Steph admired everything in the kitchen. "Check out the solarium," Sayer said to Steph gesturing to the room full of plants. Steph stuck her head in and said. "Interesting" and moved on. Sayer could not understand why that room didn't knock her socks off like it did hers. They moved into the living room. Steph looked out the doors to the lake. "Look at that view!!" Sayer said as she led her cousin through the French doors. "Good selling point," Steph remarked. Sayer started to think this was going to be harder than she thought, but then they reach the library. Steph didn't say a word just walked around touching each book with her finger. She pulled a book out "The Adventures of Tom Sawyer" opened it the front of the page. "I think this is a first edition book. It looks like there is an inscription in the book but it is so faded." She squinted her eyes as she stared at the page. "All I can make out is the letter ALS, if I am correct; this book is worth a fortune!" She put the book back and then sat down at the desk. "I love this room."

"Good, it is all yours" Sayer said.

"You don't like books?" Steph asked

"Nope, it is the plants for me," Sayer replied.

"What about cooking?" Steph asked

"Love it!!" Sayer replied with a smile on her face. Even though it has been limited to a toaster oven and a microwave.

"I do too! I love just tossing things together and seeing how it comes out." and they smiled at each other. At least they had that in common.

Steph suddenly swung around "I feel like someone is watching me!"

"Probably just my cat and here he is. Steph this is Charlie. Charlie this is Steph," Sayer introduced them. Charlie leaped off the ground and into Steph's arms. "Wow, he has never done that before. He must like you," Sayer said.

"I have never had any pets and I don't think I want to," Steph said and gently put the cat back down on the floor.

"Well, it looks like he likes you. He may have just adopted a person," Sayer said smiling but Steph looked like she just changed a dirty diaper.

"What is the rest of the house like?" She asked, while wiping her hands on her jeans.

"The upstairs has four bedrooms and a bath on each side. I took the front one on the right facing the lake. If you like that one I will move," Sayer said.

"Don't worry; I don't plan on being here long," Steph said.

"Not if I can help it," Sayer said under her breath.

Steph ended up taking the room opposite Sayer. Neither of them knew that they were taking the rooms of the two women they most took after.

Charlie took to following Steph everywhere.

Chapter 4

That evening they sat down for dinner in the dining room and had chocolate chip pancakes and strawberry milk that Sayer made. Steph observed, "It feels like such a waste using this huge room just for the two of us!"

"I agree," Sayer said. "I know dinner is not fancy, but I am used to cooking just for myself and this is all I had left when I cleaned out my cabinets. It was this or a can of sauerkraut and a piece of bread. I figured I would stock up when I find the grocery store."

"No worries. I like it. "You know what?' Steph said perking up. "I notice the small table on the porch with the two chairs that would fit in the corner of the kitchen and would be much cozier. What do you think about moving it?"

"OK," Sayer said and together they moved the small table and chairs into the kitchen. They took a step back and agreed it looked like it was made for the spot. They moved the food from the dining room to the new set up. Then they sat down to eat. "What was your mom like?" asked Steph in a shy way. She didn't know if this was something they could talk about. She knew that they would at some point, but was it too soon?

"She died when I was young. Her name was Hannah," Sayer said a matter of fact. "I almost don't remember her. What I do remember was loving and fun."

"How did she die?" Steph asked.

"A car accident on her way home from work. They say she was speeding and there was pile up and she couldn't stop fast enough. All I remember is sitting at day care as all the kids got picked up by their mom's and dad's, but no one showed up to pick me up. Not until a cop came through the door. He talked to the caretakers and then came over to me saying everything would be OK. It wasn't," Sayer said.

"That is horrible, I am so sorry. Where did you live after that?" Steph asked.

"I was in and out of foster homes until the last one. John, the father, got a tad bit too close for comfort if you know what I mean. It scared the crap out of me, so I decided there and then that I was done. So, I ran. I have been on my own since then. What about yours?" Sayer asked.

"My mom died just last year from breast cancer. I miss her terribly" Steph said with tears swelling in her eyes." She was kind and loving and always ready to talk. I never knew who my dad was, so I have been on my own too," Steph replied.

"I am sorry. That must have been tough," Sayer said. "I do not know who my dad is either."

The girls sat in silence for a moment thinking how their lives had been so different but also, in some ways, the same.

After dinner, Steph looked over the table. It was old and worn just like she loved them. "You know, I can refinish this for you."

"Sure, if you would like, I don't know how to do that sort of stuff, but I can sew so if you need a skirt or something. I can whip one up. I just need to get a machine. I sold my last one to help pay rent one month. I am also really good with plants. I plan on getting this yard in show case status. Like the solarium, you should have seen it when I got here; it was all overgrown and crazy I spent the morning working in there. There are even some plants that I have never seen before," Sayer said.

"I do not have a green thumb, but I did bring my laptop. We can look them up and while I am here I will help you get the place ready for the market," Steph said.

"I hope you change your mind," Sayer said looking at Steph. Steph could see the hope in her eyes and she felt bad that she was going to disappoint the only family she had. She said, "I have a job and an apartment back home waiting for me. I took two weeks off to get this all straightened out. I want to have a look at the will."

Sayer cleaned up from dinner while Steph got herself settled into her room.

Steph looked into all the drawers and the closet. She contemplated what could have happened to the two women who lived here, her grandmother and a great aunt that she had never heard of before. She was not the type of person to accept thing at face value, she knew she was going to figure out what the story was with her grandmother. She put her stuff in the closet on the floor and looked through all the old clothes still hanging. They all smelt like cinnamon. She loved the smell of cinnamon.

That evening Sayer looked out her bedroom window overlooking the lake. She had feeling of being at home for the first time in her life. A place that she felt she belonged. Something in the corner of her eye got her attention. She looked to the woods that abutted the property and for a moment she saw a set of glowing eyes looking at her, but at a second glance, nothing. She thought that it was her overactive imagination as a small shiver ran down her spine.

Chapter 5

After a lazy morning sitting out on the deck and in the warm sunshine with the sounds of birds in the background, choking down some instant coffee Sayer said to Steph. "This coffee is disgusting. We need to pick up something better than instant."

"I do like a good cup of coffee, but this stuff could grow hair on your chest," Steph agreed.

Laughing, Sayer dumped out her coffee and said "We should start going through the bedrooms. Maybe we will find some hints towards our history?"

"OK," Steph said. Together they went upstairs, and Sayer suggested they start in her room. First, they went to the closet and pulled the clothes out and laid them on the bed. They pulled out blouses, long skirts, and all kinds of hats and some odd cloaks. In the back, they found an old trunk, where they found some pictures. They pulled them out and spread them across the dresser.

"Do you know anyone in these pictures?" Steph asked. Sayer took them and looked at them. "Not a soul. How about you?" Sayer asked.

"Nope. No one," Steph replied.

They moved onto the Victorian dresser. It was made of dark cherry and had not a scratch on it. Steph admired the craftsmanship in the wood." The furniture in this house is remarkable," Steph said as she ran her hand over the dresser. "I have never seen such beautiful work! Every room is beautiful. The contrast with the yellow walls and the dark wood is magnificent. The delicate quilt on the bed with its soft colors goes beautifully."

They pulled the normal stuff out of the drawers like socks and pajamas, jeans, and sweaters. Sayer put her hand in the bottom drawer to pull out the last of the pants. But the edge of the pocket on the pants caught on the drawer liner and pulled it out with the pants. Sayer freed the pants and tried to put the liner back in the drawer but as she found some letters. She pulled them out and said to Steph. "Look at this." She unfolded the first, Steph looked over her shoulder and Sayer read.

Dear Sophie,

Please don't try and find us. We are safe. Isabella and I are keeping in touch. We want to have the lives that our mothers turned away from. I know you understand. You have always understood me. I want to be free from all the wacky stuff at home. I want to love and be loved. I will keep in touch.

All my love,
Hannah

"It is from your mom," Steph said to Sayer.

"I wish I knew her," Sayer said.

"Well, we are in the house she grew up in, so maybe we'll find out about her while living here," Steph said in a positive manner. It broke her heart hearing the desire in Sayers voice.

"I hope so," Sayer said. "I guess this was Sophie's room then." She continued. They found more letters. Sayer sat down to read each letter out loud as they found them.

"Listen to this," she said to Steph, who was folding tops getting ready to put them into boxes. "It looks like she fell in love with some guy name John. It says he is tall, blond and has broad shoulders. Every time he takes her out he shows up with flowers." Laughing she says." She has so many flowers that she is now putting them in beer mugs. She has run out of vases," Steph moved on to folding up the rest of the cloths and just listened to Sayer as she read the letters and talked about them. "Oh, my GODS. In this letter, she said John asked her to marry him and she said yes!" Sayer looked at Steph like it was Christmas morning. Steph couldn't help but be happy for her. Sayer never knew her mom; at least Steph knew hers for most of her life. Steph kept going through the clothes. Once everything was empty, they took all the drawers out hoping for more letters. They didn't find any. She helped Steph with the rest of the clothes. "I wonder what happened to make them want to leave," she said to Sayer.

"We will find out. Look at how much we found today. This house must be hiding the rest of the info. It looks she saved all her clothes" Steph said while holding up a pair of plaid bell bottom pants from the early '70s. "And if that is how she was about clothes; you know she will have saved more stuff that will give us hints about our moms," Steph said.

"Thank you for taking care of all these clothes. I know I was not much help," Sayer said.

"I didn't mind. I liked listening to all the letters," Steph said smiling at her cousin.

• • • • •

That evening the girls called Newt. He said he would love to come over and he would bring dinner and he could fill them in with all the details. When he showed up he just stood in the doorway staring at the girls. "You look exactly like your grandmothers. Those electric blue eyes, it is like they have their own source of energy. They looked almost like twins except for the hair. This is amazing. I wonder how much you will be like them."

The three went into the living room overlooking the lake and took their seats. Sayer said, "Why don't we eat here, and you can dish the dirt."

Steph said in a more sophisticated way "Please excuse Sayer but we would like to know everything you can tell us about our grandmothers and grandfathers since neither of us has ever meet them." Newt just started laughing and unloaded a box of fried chicken, biscuits, corn, and gravy. Just like KFC but better. He also had a copy of the will.

"More and more similarities, Sayer you seem to be like Steph's grandmother Emma. Emma was a spitfire, lots of life, and not a care in the world. She did what she wanted and how she wanted and when she wanted. Now don't get me wrong. She was not a flake. She took what she did very seriously and put everything she had into it with love. She took things as they came and dealt with them as needed. That caused lots of arguments with Sophie." Newt turned to Steph.

"Steph, you seem to be a lot like Sayer grandmother Sophie. She planned everything. She took care of the finances because; one, she loved it and second, Emma couldn't be bothered. She loved to do research as where Emma liked to experiment so in that sense they complemented each other. They would be presented with a situation and together they would find a way to fix it."

"Fix it? Like what?" Steph asked.

"Emma was into her plants and Sophie into research. For an example, sometimes someone from our community would have, let's say, a skin rash that they could not get rid of. Well they would visit your grandmothers and together, more time than not with Sophie doing the research and Emma doing the experiments, they would come up with a "cream" that would clear up the skin irritation."

"Were they homeopathic?" Steph asked.

"You could say, yes" to that, I guess. You should take a trip to Main St and check it out. They had a small booth in the back of the book store." Newt informed them.

• • • • •

Sayer looked at Steph." I think we will go tomorrow." She had a sparkle in her eye again.

"Sounds like a plan to me," Steph said and looked at Newt. "What about our grandfathers? Did you know them or our fathers?

"I don't know anything about your fathers nor your grandfathers. I never met them, and they were never mentioned. As far as I know, no man has ever lived in this house." This got Steph thinking, obviously there have been men in the lives of the O'Brien woman or they would not be here. What happened to them, and what is the story? The answers must be in this house somewhere.

• • • • •

"According to the will, Newt continued," your grandmothers wanted you both to have the house and live in the house as they did. The house has been handed down from generation of two O'Brian girls to two O'Brian girls. Sometimes they are sisters but sometimes they are cousins but always two, the house mortgage has been paid off for generations and there is a trust that has been invested and it covers the taxes and any need for upkeep. The trust will last indefinitely. With the investments that have been made, it just keeps feeding itself. I keep an eye on it.

"Can I have a look at that?" Steph asked putting her hand out.

"OK," said Newt handing the documents to Steph. He turned to Sayer with a raised eyebrow.

Sayer was jumping around doing a dance type sort of jig chanting "I am rich, I am rich, and I am rich," Steph just stared at her in stunned shock with a small smile on her face. Newt was laughing.

"Now hold on, yes there is money, but it will cover the taxes and the house up keep. You still need to make an income to cover food, electricity and if you want TV or internet. You will have to plan for the TV Company to bring it from the main road to the house. That can be expensive."

"I can live without a TV."

"I can't" growled Sayer "I love TV. Wait, does that mean you are thinking of staying?" Sayer asked Steph.

"I want to look into what happened to our grandmothers. Who our grandfathers were and why our mothers left this place. It is like my own personal mystery novel."

Sayer jumped up and began dancing again.

"You know what I noticed? They did not have a clock or a calendar. Why?" Steph asked turning to Newt while Sayer was still dancing.

"Well, they got up with the sun and to bed with the moon and they kept track of the moon cycle. I always tried to trick them into thinking it was a Christmas or New Years on the wrong day, but they always knew what day it was."

"How odd. They seem to be sort of odd," Steph said.

"Now wait a minute" Sayer interrupted. She stopped dancing and was facing Steph with fire in her eyes. They were almost glowing. Steph was staring at her with huge eyes. "How dare you. They left us this wonderful house and an opportunity to make a life. Who cares if they lived by the sun or only took a crap on the third Wednesday of each month? Who are you, oh mighty 'I have my apartment and job to get back to.' Well, I don't, and I am going to make the most of this. Go back to where ever. Don't let the door hit you butt on your way out."

Steph just stared at Sayer. Sayer had tears in her eyes and was flush with anger and her eyes were electric with anger." I am sorry, I didn't mean," Steph said.

"Shut up, whatever. I am going to bed." With that, Sayer stopped off to bed.

"That one has a temper and I thought it would have been the redhead." Newt said.

"Strawberry blond, thank you," Steph said a bit tartly.

"I think we will call it a day." Newt said as he stood up. "Let's save the rest for a different time."

Chapter 6

The next morning, as the sun was coming up, Steph went to Sayer's door and softly knocked three times.

"What?" Sayer asked through the door.

"I made you breakfast. It's out on the deck. I was rude last night, and I want to make it up to you," Steph said softly.

Sayer opened her door. Steph was surprised to see her dressed. "I smelt the bacon," Sayer said with a smile. With relief, Steph headed back down stairs.

They sat down to have their breakfast on the deck in the early morning sun. Steph was a little nervous about the fight when Sayer closed her eyes and tilted her head into the sunshine. "I will have no problem getting use to this," Steph let out her breath, relaxed and looked out at the lake.

Sayer private moment was interrupted with a frantic "Sayer look!" Sayer opened her eyes it took a few minutes for her eyes to adjust to the bright sun and looked to where Steph was pointing. Down of the beach in front of them was two of the world's biggest cats Sayer has ever seen. They were all white and the size of mid-size dogs but had ears that had small points at the ends. "They are beautiful," Sayer said.

Steph was frantic. "I know what those are, and if I am right they have wild animals slinking around this place!"

"What are they?" Sayer asked.

"Mountain lions!" Steph exclaimed while tripping over her own chair trying to get into the house.

"They are beautiful," whispered Sayer standing up to get a better view.

"They are vicious," Steph's commented. Her voice was a tad bit high.

"I wonder if I have any food for them," Sayer said calmly.

"Are you crazy? They will eat you!" Steph said with panic. She had the door just about closed, leaving just a crack open for her to talk through.

"Relax, I won't feed them," Sayer said and then "When you're around," she said under her breath. Steph closed the door and started to clean up the kitchen while Sayer stayed outside on the deck watching the cats who, in turn, were watching her. While Sayer was there admiring the beauty of the cats, one took one step forward. That broke the spell and she quickly moved inside. Steph may have point she thought.

Sayer found Steph doing the dishes, so she jumped up and sat on the counter. Steph took this as a sign that Sayer was over last night, so she commented to her. "You must have done a lot of cleaning when you first got here," Sayer told her everything was all dusty and cobwebs in every corner but she only got here the day before her.

"I started dusting and getting rid of the cobwebs and as I moved in to each room there was less and less to do so it took no time. By the time I got around to the library it looked clean enough for me," Sayer said.

Steph thought about that for a while. What is going on with this place? Something is weird. She slowly looked around the room. The walls seemed to be brighter. She shook her head.

After the dishes were done and put away, they headed up to Steph's room. Once again, they started in the closet; taking everything out, sorting it, and putting it in piles. They found more of the same clothes but no letters. "I was hoping she had kept some stuff from my mom but I knew my mom," Steph said disappointed. Once they were done they went down stairs and started examining the unknown plants. They looked at pictures on the internet until they had identified at least three. There was Mugs wart, moons locks and Mandrake. "What odd plants they have. Have you checked out the garden outside? It looks like it was rather large once upon a time," Steph said.

"I want to bring it back to life, but I don't know what it may, or may not, have in it yet. I have to wait until next spring to see what comes up," Sayer said.

As they looked around going through cupboards they found an old tattered book. "Look at this Steph said."

"What is it?" Sayer asked.

"It looks like, like a cookbook!" Steph said.

"May I please look at it?" Sayer asked, and Steph handed Sayer the book.

"Look at this, there is a recipe for acne cream, one for the influenza and one for calming the nerves. This doesn't make sense," Sayer took the book and sat down studying it. "Newt said they were like homeopathic. Maybe this is how they made all their stuff," she said.

"Are you reading?" Steph teased. Sayer just waved her hand. "You do know that is a book, right? You said you hated books and reading," Sayer ignored her. Steph continued to check out the plant room. She stuck her head out and said, "There is a lot of cat nip in here."

"Please keep the door shut," Sayer said leaving the book on the table and joining Steph in the solarium. "I keep finding Charlie in here. If we are not careful he will be stoned for life" They both started giggling.

Chapter 7

Steph got tired of looking at plants and, since she was clueless about plants anyway, she went back to the library. She got to thinking she could probably telecommute until she figured out what she wanted to do and how long she was going to be here. That way, she could take her time and figure everything out. Besides the library would make a perfect officer for her. She took a long look around the room. She loved the wall to wall shelves full of books. The desk was large and made of dark mahogany. She walked over to it and sat down in the leather seat. It was soft from years of use. She started going through the desk finding all the basics, pencils, pens, paper. In one drawer, she found a ledger book with the house expenses listed. She started studying it and then started digging for any statements of the fund that Newt told them about. No such luck. No bank statements either. The ledger stated that there was money coming in and money going out. Newt said that the trust was not large enough to support them without any other income. She wondered if they made enough at the small store for their expenses.

She looked through all the drawers but didn't come up with anything. On a bookshelf, she did find a set of photo albums. The photos were black and white, old, and yellowing but she could tell they were pictures from around this house and property. Some were of two women and two children. You could almost see the people growing up in the photos. There was a man in a lot of the pictures. The man looked like Newt. Steph took one of the photo albums and went in search of Sayer. She was no longer in the solarium, she found her outside trimming some of the ivy from around the windows. She was standing on a chair that she had dragged out from the kitchen. "Wow Sayer, you have been working hard. It is looking so tidy."

"I haven't done much just pulled a few weeds and started trimming the ivy."

"It was so overgrown just yesterday," Steph said.

"I thought so too but maybe it was the first impression effect. Now with a second look it doesn't look so bad?" She asked but it was more like a statement.

"I don't know, but I hope that it keeps up. The place is looking quite charming and will not be as hard to sell," Steph piped in.

Sayer just stared at the wall and didn't move as her heart sank. She didn't want to sell. "So, what do you want? Are you just going to constantly remind me that you don't want to stay here?"

"Sorry, please don't get mad at me again. I came out here to show you the photo album I found," Steph said to her.

"Oh," Sayer said as she climbed down off the chair. "Let's take a look." The girls sat down on the granite stoop. They started at the beginning. The first picture was of two women. One had dark hair and one with strawberry blond. They both had the piercing blue eyes. "Do you think they are our mothers?" She asked.

"Well the clothes are too old for our mothers and I would recognize mine," Steph said.

"Sorry," Sayer replied.

"It's okay. Look at this man," Steph said pointing to a man standing next to the women.

"He looks just like Newt!" Sayer said looking at Steph with a quizzical expression. "Maybe it is his dad?" she asked.

"That is what I was thinking but he looks the same as Newt does today," Steph said. The girls continued to look through the album. Sayer was just about to turn the page when Steph said, "STOP! Our moms." The girls stared at the picture.

"Are you sure?" Sayer asked

"Yup, I know my mom," Steph said.

"They look about thirteen years old! How can you be sure?" Sayer asked.

"My mom always wore her hair that way, pulled back into a side braid," Steph said with sadness in her voice.

"She is beautiful. You look like her," Sayer replied.

"Thank you," Steph said as tears were brimming in her eyes. She used her sleeve to wipe them away. Sayer put her arm around her and stared at the picture with her.

" That must be my mom," Sayer said.

"I bet it is. If you squint I can see you looking like that at thirteen," Steph said trying to lighten the mood and get her mind off her mom. They continued going page after page. Looking at birthday parties, Christmas celebrations and even what they figured were Halloween pictures. They were dressed up and it looked like they were dancing out in the night. "They look happy. I wonder why they left," Sayer asked.

"We will figure that out. Hey, is that Newt dancing with them?" Steph asked.

"It sure looks like it. What a strange guy," Sayer said.

"Well, hello there. Are you talking about me?" A male voice asked.

The girls jumped "You scared us Newt." They said in unison while laughing, as a letter fell to the ground. Steph look at Sayer and pointed to the ground. Steph bent down and recognized her mother's handwriting on the front of the envelopes. She scooped them up. Smiling she said, "Hey, is this you in the pictures?"

"Sure is," he said.

"What about these of our grandmother?" Sayer asked.

"Yup that is me," he replied.

"How do you stay looking so young?" Steph inquired.

"Let's just say good genes," he replied.

"Dang I want your genes," Sayer said.

"Careful what you wish for." Newt says with a sad smile.

"What brings you around?" Steph asked him.

"I just wanted to check and see how you girls are doing. Is everything going okay? Are you settling in alright? Do you have any questions for me?"

"We have lots of questions. You want to join us for lunch?" Steph offered.

"Sure, I would love too. I only have a few minutes. I am on my way into town" He informed them.

"I hope you like peanut butter and jelly. We still need to go to the store," Sayer said.

"That is one of my favorites," he said smiling.

Sayer went into the kitchen to make the sandwiches. The trio went out on the deck to have lunch. They all sat down, and Sayer started putting potato chips in her sandwich. She looked up to staring eyes of Steph and Newt. "What?"

"What are you doing to your sandwich?" Newt asked.

"You have never put chips in your sandwich? It is one of the finer things in life. Try it!" Sayer replied.

Steph and Newt opened their sandwiches and put one chip in. Closed it. Steph said, "Here goes nothing," and takes a bite. Her eyes lit up. Newt saw her expression and did the same. The two of them put more chips in their sandwiches.

"I had never thought of this?" Newt said with a mouth full and chip dust falling out.

"You should try Munchos in tuna. It is to die for," Sayer said.

"Interesting," Steph replied without enthusiasm; but from that day forward, all sandwiches had chips in them.

• • • • •

"So, Newt," Sayer said with her mouth full. "How far does our family go back on this land?"

"Back to the 1600s" He replied between bites.

"So, the china in the dining room is the original china of the house?" Steph asked in awe.

"I believe it is. It is valuable china. Be careful with it." He cautioned them.

"We will be," Sayer said and turning to Steph she said, "We are not selling it."

"Don't worry; I was not going to suggest that," Steph said as innocently as she could.

The three of them sat around and continued talking into mid afternoon.

• • • • •

After Newt had left, Steph sat with cups of tea for each of them at the small table in the kitchen. She pulled out the stack of letters. Sayer cleaned the up the lunch dishes while Steph read her mother's letter out loud.

Dear Emma,

I am enjoying school to the fullest. I have made plenty of friends. Don't worry I am not making any stupid mistake. I have found my psychology class to be the most intriguing class. The professor is brilliant, and he even takes time outside of his classes to help those who have extra interest is the field. I am seriously thinking of switching my major. His name was Professor Joseph Smith. He has dark hair and is very handsome with in his glasses and tie. I need to go and study in the library I will write again soon.

Lots of love,
Isabella

Steph folded the letter and skimmed over the next letter.

"Listen to this," Steph said. "She started to date the professor!"

"No way!" Sayer said as she refreshed Steph's tea "She was the wild one."

"They planned on getting married and she was very excited when she got pregnant," Steph continued.

"Did your mother tell you they were getting married?" Sayer asked.

"Yes. She told me he was the love of her life, but she left out the part that he was her teacher," Steph said smiling at Sayer.

"What happened to him?" Sayer asked.

"She said he just up and left one day, and when I asked her if she wanted to look for him she always said' 'no' and she always got sad about it, so I didn't ask too often," Steph said.

"We now have a name to work with," Sayer said wiggling her eyebrows at Steph.

"We have two and a half names. It is a start," Steph said laughing.

Chapter 8

The next day the girls took Steph's car into town. It did not take long to find Main St. It looked like a picture perfect old New England Main street. It was a wide street with big maple trees and street lamps for the evenings. At one end was a brick building with the town offices, police station, and fire station side by side. The other end of Main Street featured the town library that looked like a castle with tall windows and towers on the ends. In between the two were all kinds of small boutiques, cafes, smoke shops, and a coffee house. Nested in the middle was the book store.

Steph slowed way down as they approached the store.

"Isn't it just darling?" Steph asked.

"Looks like a store to me," Sayer said. Steph gave Sayer a sideway glance. "What? It is a store, not a puppy," Sayer said smiling at Steph.

They parked the car in front of the shop. "Let's check it out?" Steph said.

"Let's get a coffee first, a real one. "Sayer replied, pointing to the café next door to the bookstore.

"OK," Steph said giving in easily.

"We can get some real coffee beans while we are here," Sayer informed her.

They went into "A Cup of Joe." "I hope the coffee is better than the name," Sayer murmured. The place had a half dozen high top table and advertised free Wi-Fi. The walls were covered with pictures of coffee beans.

Most of the tables were full and you could hear the chatter of people talking and the clicking of computer keys as they walked in; but once they took three steps inside you could have heard a pin drop.

"It feels like we are the new kids in school," Sayer mumbled under her breath. Steph gave her a sideway punch with her elbow. They walked up to the counter. Sayer said, "I will take a small iced coffee, caramel swirl, extra half ice." The young man behind the counter had sandy brown hair and green eyes, square jaw and gave her a smile and said "This is not Dunkin Donuts but, since you are new, I will let it slide. I know what you mean but, just so you know, we put Dunkin into shame, I will set you up." He had a deep voice that could make your knees weak. He kept his eyes on Sayer but spoke to Steph "What would you like?

"I would like a medium regular please."

"OK. Will there be anything else," he said while keeping his eyes on Sayer only glancing down a few times while making the coffees.

Steph replied, "No thank you." She couldn't help but notice the interest this man had in Sayer.

"Where are you from Blue eyes?" The guy asked Sayer while he continued making their drinks. The clatter of the café had picked up.

"I am from Chicago," Sayer told him.

"I am from New Hampshire," Steph piped in, but she didn't think he was listening to her.

"How long you going to be in town?" Nick asked.

"We just moved here my cousin and I," Sayer said and gestured to Steph. "Our grandmothers have passed, and they left us house out on the lake." The coffee shop went completely silent again. The guy at the counter stared at her.

"Do you mean the old O'Brian house?" he asked.

"Yup that's the one," Sayer hesitantly replied. Steph slowly turned around and saw that everyone was looking at them.

He handed them their coffees and winked at Sayer "I should've known by your eyes. I used to see your grandmother's every day when they came in for coffee." He looked at Steph then back to Sayer and said "The coffees are on the house. Welcome to the neighborhood. "

"Thank you?" Sayer took to a sip then closed her eyes and took a long drink. "Oh, this is so much better. Thank you. Can we get a bag of beans to go?"

"Any time, Blue eyes," Nick said. He didn't even glance at Steph.

While Sayer was in her coffee nirvana, Steph asked turning back to the counter "Is something wrong?" She asked leaning forward and in a whisper.

"Nope, just ignore them, they are just nosey. We don't get a lot of new people moving to town," Nick said to her.

They said, "Thank you" on the way out the door. Sayer turned around. "What is your name?"

"Nick."

"It is nice to meet you, Nick," Sayer said. Nick winked at Sayer and smiled as he watched the girls walk down the sidewalk.

"Well, someone has a crush on you?" Steph said to Sayer.

"Shut up," said Sayer, but she was smiling.

"He called you blue eyes not me and we have the same eyes!"

"Mine are bigger."

"No, they are not," Steph said giggling.

Chapter 9

The cousins walked next door to the bookstore. As Steph stepped through the door, a set of wind chimes made a soothing medley and she took a deep breath. She was enveloped with the smell of paper and leather.

"Smells like a school library," Sayer muttered wrinkling up her nose.

"Hey, you got your fancy coffee give me this. OK?" Steph said.

"Touché," Sayer replied.

The shop was surprisingly large. One side was full of children's books; everything a child could read or be read to. The other side had history books, cookbooks to self-help books, even books on how to books.

The counter by the door was empty. "I will be with you in a moment!" they heard come from the back of the room.

"Nice security," Sayer said.

"Do you always do that?" Steph asked.

"Do what?" Sayer asked innocently.

"Make a wise comment everywhere you go?" Steph asked.

"Yup, it my motto," Sayer said with a smile on her face.

"Oh my GOD! Welcome home! I am so happy to see you!" They were suddenly being hugged again and again by this bubbly blond woman."

"Um, who are you?" Sayer asked; her arms pinned to her side by this stranger.

"Oh my God. I am sorry! I am Anne. I am, or was, a good friend of your grandmothers. I own the book store, and I just know you will love having your shop here just like they did." Anne looked to be in her mid-fifties with just a few gray hairs. She was short and plump. She had deep laugh lines around her eyes. You could tell that she was always smiling.

"That is why we are here. We wanted to find out about it," Steph said. "Newt told us about the store yesterday."

"What, don't you know? Let me show you. Give me a moment," she said turning around to the door. "And I will lock up and show you around. I have kept everything the same. I knew you would come back and take over. It is your heritage. Plus, your grandmothers said you would. How could you not?" Anne bounced towards the back end of the store; talking non-stop. Steph and Sayer looked at each other with question marks in their eyes and started to follow her. Sayer made the sign of a crazy person next to her head. Steph batted her hand down and mouthed "STOP!"

In the back end of the store there was a display counter with cards, cans of incense and some shelves with books.

"I sold what I could, so I have some cash for you. They rest of the stuff I put into storage until you got here and decided to get back into business."

"What is all this?" Sayer said gestured to a display of books about stars, how to read your future in tea leaves. There were crystals hanging on a rack. "So, they sold crap and made a living?" Sayer asked. Turning in a circle looking around at what she considered worthless junk. Her heart sank down to her knees.

"No!" Ann said with a sort of confused expression on her face. "This is just the stuff that they didn't make themselves. They sold all kinds of creams, teas and herbs and tinctures that they made."

"Remember. Newt said they were Homeopaths," Steph said.

"No. They were witches and so are you!" Anne continued without missing a beat. "They made this fabulous hand cream that could cure any dry skin in a flash. It sold like hot cakes. They had a tea that the local kids swear would clear up acne." Anne informed them.

Sayer interrupted Anne "They.... Hold on! You are said our grandmothers were witches? Sayer threw her arms up in the air "This is UN-freaking believable." I finally have an opportunity for a life, and you say I have inherited a freaking crazy house."

"I had a feeling," Steph said quietly.

"What?" Sayer asked looking at Steph with shock and anger. "When were you going to tell me?" Sayer asked loudly. Her face was turning red and the sun must have been hitting her eyes because they seemed to have a soft glow to them like they did the other night.

"Well, look at all the strange plants," Steph said, calmly trying to defuse Sayers anger but she couldn't help but stare at her eyes. "Remember that book you found with all the odd stuff you could do with those plants? Moon leaves or whatever it was called? Tiger root? Not Basil and parsley," Steph said. Sayer just glared at her, turned and walked out.

Steph knew by now that you should let Sayer cool off, so she stayed behind to talk to Anne.

Steph said, "Sorry about that. She has a temper."

"I am not surprised. Remember, I knew your grandmothers. I loved them dearly." Anne said.

"We got strange looks in the coffee shop," Steph said quietly wondering if they were going to be considered freaks. "What do you know about this stuff?" Steph asked Anne.

"Not much, your grandmothers did it all. They always concentrated on only doing things of a positive nature. They always said that all magic has a price. If you do good magic it will cost in a good way. If you do anything that can go negative the cost will be negative. You know what I mean? "

"Basically, you get back what you put out," Steph said.

"In a nutshell," Anne replied.

"I do not plan on staying in the area. I want to fix up the house and sell it," Steph told Anne.

"You can't do that. The house will not let you." Anne said.

"The house will not let me? What do you mean?" Steph asked.

"That house has been an O'Brian house since the beginning. It is said that the house chose the O'Brian's." Anne said.

"How can a house choose a family?" Steph asked.

"I don't know but that is the legend. It always goes to two girls." Anne said. "It is just something everyone knows."

Steph was beginning to agree with Sayer, thinking the whole town was crazy. "Um. I must go and check on Sayer. I will see you soon," Steph said and with a wave and she was out the door in a flash.

Anne watched her leave, thinking that it should have gone so much better. Shaking her head, she went to the door and reversed the sign to open and went over to the children's department to tidy up a bit.

Steph found Sayer outside leaning up against the car drinking a second coffee. "You better slow down on that stuff," Steph said to her.

"Call it therapy. Let's just go home," Sayer grumbled.

The ride was a quiet one, with each girl lost in her own thoughts.

As they pulled up to the house, Steph noticed the house could use a coat of paint around the trim and the lawn still needed mowing. She made a mental note to put it on her to do list.

• • • • •

Sayer thought about the potions book, and the plants, and what she may be able to make for herself. She felt sorry for herself. She didn't want to be the town crackpot. She didn't have anywhere else to go. This was it. It was all she had. Sayer escaped to her room. She needed to think.

Chapter 10

Steph grabbed the current book she was reading and headed out to the deck.

When she got involved in a book, she tended to forget her surrounding and become deaf to the world. At one point, she put the book down on her lap and put her head back and rested her eyes. When she opened them, she jumped, yelled "Oh My God!" and ran in the house, locked the door, pulled down the curtain and ran up the stairs to Sayer's room, and pounded on her door out of breath.

"What?" Sayer groaned through the door.

"That mountain lion, panther thing was on the deck staring at me. It was licking its chops and was growling. It almost made me it's dinner," Steph shrilled in full panic mode.

"What?" Sayer said. She threw open the door and ran down the stairs.

"Sayer what are you doing? We need to call animal control. Sayer! Sayer! What are you doing? Don't let it in," Steph yelled behind Sarah, almost in tears.

"I am not going to let them in, so do not worry, but they are so cool." The girls stood inside the glass door watching the cat. The next moment the other one joined it. The cats sat on the railing of the deck watching the girls peeking out at them from behind the curtain. Then at once on cue they both jumped up onto the roof.

"Now what are we going to do?" Steph asked.

"What do you mean? They just left," Sayer said.

"No, they are on the roof waiting for their snacks to come out and play," Steph said.

Sayer started to laugh. Let's make dinner. You know what? We never went to the store."

The girls had takeout, inside. Steph was too scared to go on the deck. She hoped that by the morning the cats would be gone. Over dinner Sayer brought the topic up, "You know Steph, I have been looking through that plant book and I am going to try and make some of those ointments. I want to see if I have any talent with it. I am not saying I am a witch, but I can follow instructions."

"No harm in trying. What do you think of the witch stuff?" Steph asked.

"I don't know but I bet that is why our mothers left and didn't tell us about our grandmothers. They knew they were crazy," Steph replied.

"I agree but, there is a lot of odd stuff around this place. I have been doing some research on this place and our family," Steph said. "When?" Sayer asked.

"On my laptop, last night in bed. Only O'Brian women have lived in this house for over 100 years," Steph continued. "There is no mention of any men."

"We have two names don't forget," Sayer said.

"We should ask Newt about it," Sayer said

"Agreed. What?' Steph said.

"I said we should ask Newt about it," Sayer said.

"NO after that," Steph asked.

"I didn't say anything else" Sayer said.

"I thought I heard something like you whispered a comment," Steph said.

"You're hearing things," Sayer said.

"I think I am. I keep hearing whispering. Have you heard it?" Steph asked between bites.

"No, and this place is not haunted if that is the angle you are going with," Sayer said.

"No, I just keep hearing voices," Steph said.

"That is not a good sign. You know what they say about hearing voices," Sayer said with a smirk on her face.

"I think I am just kind of freaked out about everything and my imagination is getting away from me," Steph said stretching her arms up over her head. "I am going to hit the hay. I will see you in the morning."

Sayer looked out the window and noticed that the sun was setting. She decided to go to bed too. She had a feeling that they were going to be up early.

Chapter 11

The next morning Steph watched the sun rise from her room. She was never up this early, but she felt refreshed. She went down stairs and found that Sayer was already up too.

"You're up early," Steph said stifling a yawn as she walked into the kitchen.

"I couldn't sleep any more. I have a lot going through my head that I need to sort out. How about you? Why are you up so early?" she asked handing a cup of coffee to Steph.

"I think the sun was shining on my face and it woke me up. That room is bright in the morning. No wonder our grandmothers were always up early. They didn't have a choice with the sun shining through those doors and windows."

"I bet you are right. Let's make the best of it and go into town and get those groceries and maybe we can avoid any odd looks," Sayer suggested.

They got dressed and Sayer waited outside by the car and cracking up at Steph's antics. She darted from behind one object to the next in a zigzag pattern to get to the car. She looked like a ninja leaving the house. A bad ninja! "What are you doing?" Sayer said laughing.

"I am keeping an eye out for those mountain lions."

"Just get in the car," Sayer said chuckling.

• • • • •

When they got into town, Sayer got another coffee from "A Cup of Joe" but a different guy waited on them. Sayer left a little disappointed. She was hoping to see Nick again. They picked up some groceries and stopped at the hardware store and picked up a few gallons of paint for the house and some boxes. They were back to the house within a few hours.

Steph ran back and forth from the car to the house trying to get everything unloaded as fast as she could; while Sayer calmly took her time. Newt came walking up the street "Hey girls. How's it going?"

"Hi Newt. How are you?" Sayer asked. He replied, "I'm pretty," Sayer looked at him, confused by his reply and continued "We have lots of questions for you. We went to the store our grandmothers had," Sayer said standing in the driveway.

Newt looked at them with a raised eyebrow. "And?"

"Anne told us that they were witches?" Sayer said.

"Ayah, and what do you think?" Newt asked.

"I don't know. You don't seem surprised," Steph said coming to join them.

" I'm not because it is true. Your grandmothers were wonderful witches?"

"Like Glinda the good witch or the wicked witch of the west?" Sayer asked.

Laughing Newt said, "Glenda but not so fairy like."

"Did you see that?" Steph asked, "I just thought I saw something move."

"It must have been some leaves. "Sayer said rolling her eyes.

"What do you think about all this?" Newt asked her.

Steph kept glancing in every direction. Not looking at anyone. "I want to learn about my history while I am here. Can we talk inside?" She started walking towards the door, not waiting for them. "I have set up things at my job, so I can telecommute for a while. It is a temporary situation, but it should give me time to figure out what I want to know. I swear I just saw s something moving let's get into the house. Move it, will you?"

"Now you sound paranoid," Sayer said following her.

"Let's get inside I don't want those mountain lions sneaking up on me again," Steph said, as she was waited to close the door.

"Mountain lions?" Newt asked.

"She is referring to the mountain lions we have seen around the place," Sayer told Newt.

"Oh," Newt said with a smile and a glint in his eyes.

They walked through the front door. All the woodwork was gleaming and the floors shining," Sayer did you do this?" Steph asked.

"No. How could I? I was with you all day."

"Then how did it get so clean?" Steph asked.

"It is the house." Newt said. They both turned to look at him like he had six heads.

"Ann said something about the house," Steph said. "Houses do not clean themselves."

Newt kept his mouth shut. He knew the time would come and they would begin to believe.

As they walked around to the living room, they found two books on the coffee table. One was a journal with the history of the O'Brien family. The second was huge, brown, and thick. The cover just had a crest symbol on it.

"Now that is freaky," Sayer stated.

Newt sat down. "The house has a way of knowing what you need and, if it can, it will supply you with it. You have to be careful because it also takes stuff away."

"So, if I say I want a grill cheese it will make me one?" Sayer asked.

"No, nothing like that. Like these books. The house feels it is time for you to have them. You never know what to expect," he said.

"Wow. That is what Anne was talking about. Do we get to fly brooms?" Sayer asked. She was beginning to like the idea of being a witch and having a magical house.

"No" said Newt chucking making his big belly jiggle. "That is only in story books."

"What sort of stuff can we do?" Steph asked.

"You can do just about anything but remember every ounce of magic come with a price. Small magic, small price, big magic, big price. You also need to remember the meaning behind magic because what you do to others comes back to you threefold. Always keep that in mind."

"Now what is your real story Newt? Why did you look the same in all those pictures? Steph asked him.

"I am an alchemist. I have found a way to slow down the aging process." He informed them.

"I thought alchemy was changing metal into gold," Steph asked relaxing in to the couch across from him.

"That is one part, but I have not been successful with." he said with a sad sigh.

"That is cool. How old are you?" Sayer asked.

"Let's talk about that later." Newt said.

Steph asked Newt "Do people think we are crazy?"

"No, the exact opposite. The town loves having your family here" Newt replied. "Then why did everyone stop talking in the cafe when we entered it?" Steph asked him.

"That is a good question, but I bet is because you are the new witches in town and they don't know what to think of you." Newt said.

"I wonder," Steph said tapping her finger to her chin thinking.

Sayer looked through the book. She felt less and less confident that she would be able to do anything from the book. "This looks so confusing. I think these are spells. I don't know if I can do this. "Sayer said with a wrinkled brow looking at the book. "It is like foreign language."

"You girls need to discover what you are able to do and how to control it." Newt told them.

" How are we supposed to do that? Who will teach us?" Sayer asked looking up from the book.

"In the past, they learned from their mothers or grandmothers but since yours moved away and they passed before you returned, I don't know." The three of them sat there in thought for a moment. Newt looked up out on the deck and noticed two cats looking in. "Oh, they have returned," he said. Steph head turned to the door and she screamed and jumped up on the sofa and then behind it. She crouched close to the floor. "Oh my GOD, oh my God, oh my God." She cried.

"Are these the mountain lions you were talking about?" Newt asked.

“Yes,” Sayer said while peeking over the back to the couch to look at Steph on the floor.

“They are your grandmother’s cats.” Newt said nonchalantly, like everyone has wild animals for pets.

Steph and Sayer exclaimed “What?” They said in unison. Steph popped her head over the back of the couch to look out the door. Then she ducked back down.

“These cats were always with them except when they went into town. They are lynx cats. People would freak out when they saw the cats they were not too good for business.”

“You think?” said Sayer. “So, they are friendly?” she asked.

“No, not friendly. They were very loving to your grandmothers but watch out if you are a stranger. They were with your grandmothers all the time and they are probably wondering who you are.” Newt said.

“No kidding,” Sayer said.

“Give it time they may like you too.” Newt said.

“No way. They can go back to the mountains,” Steph exclaimed.

“I’ll give them some milk.” was Sayer reply.

“What? No don’t do that! Don’t encourage them,” Steph was just about screaming, kneeling behind the couch looking over the back with her hands over her mouth and wide eyes.

“Stop being a sissy,” Sayer got up and went into the kitchen.

“I don’t know how well giving them milk is going to work. I have never been around them without your grandmother’s.” Newt said. And with that the two cats jumped up back to the roof.

“Thank God,” Steph sighed. Sayer came out of the kitchen but not with any milk but with two sticks.

“What’s that?” Steph asked happy not to see milk in her hands.

” I think they are wands,” Sayer said.

“You’ve got to be kidding me,” Steph said rolling her eyes.

” Nope that is what they are. They belonged to your grandmothers. They have been handed down with the house for many generations. The house must have had them.” Newt informed them.

“If no one has seen them, then how did the house get them?” Steph asked.

"Good question." Newt replied.

"How do we use these?" Sayer asked sticking it in the air and tricking a pose.

"They are basically just sticks but if you have the gift you can channel your power through them. Makes it easier to direct it to where you want." Newt said.

"Can you use any stick?" Sayer asked.

"In theory, I guess." He replied with a shrug.

Steph got up and picked up one of the wands. She started to twirl it in the air like Sayer. They were making funny faces, striking possess and giggling. the air in the room began to lighten. Newt started to laugh along with the girls. Sayer spun around, her hair fell out of her pony tail. It was flying around her as she kept spinning and laughing, spinning, and laughing, twirling, and twirling. Steph stopped and watched her along with Newt. Sparks started to shoot out of her wand, twirling and laughing, twirling, and laughing. Then there was a bang and a crash as one of the oil lamps fell off the shelf. Steph and Newt dived for cover. Sayer was breathless with a wild look in her eyes and they were glowing. "That was awesome," she said, standing there breathing deep.

"Sayer your eyes!?" Steph exclaimed as she pulled herself up off the floor.

"What about them?" Sayer asked. She put her hands over her eyes. When she put her hands back down her eyes looked normal again.

• • • • •

"It must have been the light hitting them they were glowing and that was amazing! It was powerful!" Steph said." I could feel your energy. It was building and building while we were spinning. I had to stop. It was getting too much for me, but you seemed just to channel it like a natural."

"I could feel it going through my blood. It was the most wonderful thing," Sayer said as she collapsed back onto the couch.

"You need to be careful. Look at what you did to the oil lamp." Newt gestured to the broken lamp on the floor.

"Oh yah. That is not good," Sayer said as she got back up and went looking for a broom and dustpan. Steph turned to Newt, "We need to figure this out. Sayer looks like she is going to be good at this."

Chapter 12

The next day Steph got up with the sun. As she walked down the stairs she saw Sayer outside on the deck. She was dressed in jeans and a blouse. Her hair was wild and when she turned around Steph noticed the dark makeup around her eyes. “Going goth?”

“Just the mood I woke up in. What do you want to do today?” she said.

“I want to start to figure out what we can do, if anything?” Steph said.

“Oh good,” Sayer said with relief in her voice. “Let’s go down to the beach and play with these.” Holding out the wands.

“Okay, but I don’t know where we are going to start,” Steph went inside to get something for breakfast. She noticed Sayer bringing in two bowls.” Did you have company this morning?”

“Um, yup.”

“Who?”

‘Let’s say, just some neighbors,” Steph looked at her quickly. Sayer had a strange look in her eye and didn’t push it.

Steph went into the kitchen to make herself some breakfast. When she came into the kitchen there was a small book on the table. She picked it up and read the title. “Control”

Steph took the book back out to the deck. “Well the house has given us some help.”

"What do you mean?" Sayer asked.

"I just found this small book on the table." It is called "Control" Steph said.

"Why don't we take the other book with us too? Where did you put it?" Sayer said.

"I didn't put it anywhere. I left it in the living room," Steph said. They searched all over the place for it.

"Newt said the house will take stuff. That is so freaking strange," Steph stated.

"It's cool," Sayer replied.

The girls walked down the hill towards the beach. The lawn was nice and thick with grass and had a fire pit in the middle and what looked to be an old, neglected garden to the left and some ancient picnic tables on the right. It wasn't a huge area but plenty of room for a cookout with friends; if they made any. The beach itself was all sandy and the water got deep gradually.

• • • • •

Steph opened the book and started to read out loud.

"It is very important to be able to control the power within. Without control the power can take over and control the witch. Close your eyes and clear your mind. With your inner eye, picture a small portion of sand swirling turning clockwise up off the ground. Start with a small circle and slowly make it larger, going around and around and slowly bringing it up into the air.

Okay, Sayer," Steph stopped speaking mid word and stared at Sayer. She had a cloud of sand spinning in the air above her head. He eyes were closed, and her chin pointed into the air. Faster and faster the cloud spun. Steph was just amazed. It was a sight to see. Bits of sand started to tickle Steph's nose and before she could help herself she let out a loud sneeze; startling Sayer and breaking her concentration; and then the sand started to rain down. Sayer yelled "OW" and put her arms over her head.

"Holy cow! How did you do that?" Steph asked.

"I just did what you said to do. You try it," Sayer said brushing some sand off herself and putting her hand out for the book

Steph stood up, pointed her wand at the ground, closed her eyes and started to rotate her wand in small circles. "Am I doing it?"

"Nope, not even any dust."

Steph was concentrating so hard her forehead was all creased and still nothing. She kept trying for another ten minutes and nothing. "Why isn't this working?"

"I think you are trying too hard. Shake your arms out, jump up and down; rotate your head a few times. Displace the stress. Do some jumping jacks. Wave your arms up and down. Scratch your butt."

Steph stopped and looked at Sayer who was cracking up. "You were doing everything I said I wanted to see how far I could go." She was laughing so hard she had started crying. Steph started to laugh too just the mental image she got was cracking her up. Once they calmed down Steph tried again. This time it started to work. She got so excited; she lost her concentration and had to start again. Once she got the hang of it, the two of them did it together and with both of them it became a full-blown sand storm. When they were done they looked at the book for the next step. Their excitement was so powerful it felt like static in the air. The book instructed them to do the same thing but with water.

This time it wasn't as easy for Sayer as it was with the sand. It took her three tries to get the water up into the air and maintain it for a period of time. Steph could do it on the first try. When the two of them tried to do it together it looked like the beginning of a water spout. They decided not to continue to try that one together. Steph thought, "If it got out of control it could be a disaster."

"Let's call it quits for the day. I am exhausted. It takes a lot out of you," Sayer said to Steph.

"Good idea." looking at her watch Steph said. "Wow, we have been at this for hours."

As the girls started to walk back up the hill Sayer looked up at the house and stopped. "Steph doesn't it look like there is a third floor?" Steph looked up at the house and, sure enough, it looked like there was a small deck and a door above the bedroom windows.

" Let's go find a way up there." They ran the rest of the way up the hill into the house. They found two bottles of water waiting for them on the counter. Sayer just shrugged at Steph and grabbed one. "I am beginning to like having the house in charge," Sayer handed one to Steph. "Let's go upstairs and see what we can find."

The two girls climbed the stairs to the second floor. They started in the bedrooms looking for any way to a third floor. They looked in closets for concealed doors. Checked out the ceiling, for a drop-down attic door. They even looked in all the closets for a crawl space to go through and found nothing. Steph sat down on one of the beds. "How do think you get up there?" she asked Sayer.

"Maybe you need to use a ladder?" was Sayer reply.

"That would be one tall ladder and I don't like heights," Steph said.

"Add it to the list of questions for Newt," Sayer sat down next to Steph. "There is so much to figure out. I do hope you stick around long enough to help me."

"Don't worry. I will help you. This is fun," Steph said as she laid back and joined Sayer. The both sat there in their own thoughts, staring at the ceiling.

Chapter 13

Sayer woke up with a jolt and sat straight up. She had fallen asleep on the bed with Steph, but a noise woke her up. She heard it again. It was a cat call. A wild cat call, "Steph did you hear them?"

"What?" Steph said stifling a yawn. "The cats!" Sayer got up and ran down stairs with Steph slowly following behind. It was dawn and the sun was just beginning to peak over the horizon.

"What time is it? I think we slept through the night!" Steph asked.

"I don't know," Sayer said with a shrug. "We laid down and fell asleep. It happens like that." They walked down stairs and opened the door to the deck to watch the sunrise. Sayer was just about to take a step but jumped back. She had almost stepped on a dead squirrel. "Gross! How did that get there? Oh my god, there are two!!"

"And a mouse" Steph was saying while yawning. "I need coffee. I am going in to make some."

"Steph there are dead vermin on our porch," Sayer exclaimed angrily.

"Yup. I will start the coffee and you get rid of them" Steph said.

Sayer went inside and got a broom and a small shovel from next to the fire place. She went out and scooped up the first rodent then walked to the side yard to dispose of it. But then she looked up into a tree and jumped back. There, staring down at her, were three sets of cat eyes. Two large and one set of small eyes. The lynx cats were watching her from the tree with Charlie sitting between them. Sayer began to laugh. She walked back into the house got three bowls of milk and went back to the deck. She was first greeted by Charlie. Who was purring and wrapping himself around her legs. She put the bowls down and sat on the deck cross legged to pet her kitty. The next thing she knew, there were three cats rubbing against her and purring loudly. She just sat there laughing. Steph came out with a look of horror on her face. "It's ok Steph!! It is not growling like you thought; they are purring!!" They were almost pushing her over with affection. Steph slowly opened the door. One of the cats walked in and rubbed itself around her legs. She carefully reached down to pet it." Oh, she is so soft," Steph walked outside and joined her cousin. Together they sat on the deck with the three cats, who continued drinking the milk while they watched the sun fully rise in the sky. Then the cats walked in the house together and all curled up on the couches and went to sleep. Sayer turned to Steph. "I think they have moved in."

"I get that feeling too," Steph said. "I wonder what their names are."

"I bet Newt knows" Sayer replied.

"What doesn't he know?" Steph said with a smirk on her face shaking her head.

"I am going to play with the plants. At least now we know why there is so much cat nip." Sayer said

Steph spent the morning going through the journals in the library. She got back to learning that the men in the family either did not last long or were simply never even mentioned. Some of her ancestors had been married but the spouses always disappeared or died and early death. The woman in the family changed their names back to O'Brian or never changed it when they got married. A few said the O'Brien family is cursed when it comes to love. Steph started to draw out a family tree. She hoped to fill in the blank names of all the men. There had to be a record somewhere. She started to go through all the books. She was thinking and hoped that some information could be hidden in a book. As she pulled books off the shelf and gave them a shake; she found a book that was not a book. It was a lever disguised as book. When she pulled the lever forward a door open in the wall. Steph stared at it open mouth then ran to get Sayer.

• • • • •

"Sayer come quick you have to see this," she said while running to find Sayer.

Sayer pooped her head out of the solarium. "What?"

"I found a hidden door," Steph said with her eyes wide excitement "Come on. Put that down. Let's see where it goes," Steph's face was flushed. She grabbed Sayers shirt and dragged her to the library. "Maybe it will bring us up to the third floor." That is not where it took them. The door opened to a stairway going down and each step it would light up; lighting the way. Steph turned to Sayer "This is way too cool." As they climbed down the stairs the air got cooler and you could smell damp earth. At the bottom, the hall went in different directions. The cats had followed them down and now lead them to a door at the far end of the hallway. Steph looked at the cats. "I think they want us to go through that door," Steph pushed on the door and it slowly opened. The cats left and went back upstairs. The girls stepped through the doorway and their jaws dropped. It was so full you couldn't tell where one thing started and the other ended. "I think they were hoarders," Sayer said to Steph.

"Look at this stuff it is not just old newspapers. There are caldrons, bottles, and other stuff. I bet it is a storage room. Who knows what we will find in here."

The two girls started to paw through the boxes. Lots of old clothes, books, magazines, Christmas ornaments, Halloween decoration. If you could name it, it most likely would be able found in this room. They spent an hour just looking through the boxes. Sayer was hoping to find information about her mom. Steph just wanted information.

"Look at this," Sayer handed Steph a photo album. She had finally found something she thought would be useful. It was full of pictures of men.

"Oh my. I think we found a record of the men. I am bringing this upstairs," Steph said

"Don't you want to see where the rest of the hallways go?" Sayer asked her.

"Later," Steph said as she was walking back up the stairs, so Sayer followed her up.

She went back up to the library. Steph put the book leaver back in the upright position to close the door. They opened the book on the desk. Each picture had a name and birthdate and death day. It was like a tomb stone.

"This is sad," Sayer flipped the pages to the back there we two pictures of men. One had the name John Giles. He had dark hair and blue eyes. The other had the name Joseph Smith. He had blond hair and green eyes.

"Our dads," Steph said. "At least they don't have their death dates listed."

"Wow. That is cool," Sayer said. "Now we have more info to work with." They left the photo album on the desk and went back to the living room lost in thought. Steph grabbed her laptop, and the minute her butt hit the couch her keyboard started clicking.

"I wonder what happened to them or where they are. Maybe we can find them," Sayer said.

"We are going to try that is for sure," Steph said while she was working on her computer.

Chapter 14

For the next several days the girls spent their time practicing with the wind and water and earth as instructed in the "Control Book." They Worked on getting things together for the store and researched the names they had discovered. Steph did a Google search on each of the names and had lots of hits. She narrowed her search with the little information that they had; only birth dates; and she had hit a dead end.

Early the next morning, Newt came around. He was greeted by all three cats. "I see the cats have moved back in." He had a bag of cat treats.

The girls were very happy to see him. "What are the cat's names?" Sayer asked him while wiping her hands on her apron. "This one is Andromeda, gesturing to the cat with very smooth sleek fur, and the one with the fluffy white fur is Cassiopeia," he said.

"Oh, those are names of constellation. I will look up the meanings," Steph said as she pulled out her phone.

Sayer turned to Newt. "I have been working with some of the recipes in that old tattered book. I have found these things called "Medicine bags."

"Yes, I am familiar with them. Have you been successful?" He asked.

"Yes, I think so. There seems to be different one for each need. Some are for anxiety, some for strength, and some for love. You just put the different ingredients in leather pouches; say some crazy words and poof. They will have the acquired effect needed. We can sell them in the store," Sayer was saying.

"Did you make them under the full moon?" Newt asked

"No, why?" Sayer asked.

"I believe to have full power they need to be made under the full moon," Newt informed her.

"Oh," Sayer had a look of disappointment on her face. She left the room and came back with the book. She started to flip through the pages. She found the one she wanted and notice a drawing of the moon on the top of the page. "I guess it is not as straightforward as I thought. I will just toss the ones I made in the trash."

"No need to do that! Use them as display items. Make some new ones when the moon is full to sell. Consider it was a practice run" Newt suggested.

"That is an excellent idea!" Steph said walking back into the room.

"Our family has been doing this stuff for ever. We just need to follow their lead. We will get the hang of it. Oh," Sayer said full of excitement jumping up and down waving her hands in the air. "You want to know what I almost did this morning. You know how we were working with the wind the other day? I almost made my bed with my wand. I swear I saw the blanket twitch," Sayer eyes were bright, and her mood had perked up at the memory of this morning.

"Sayer, you are amazing. You have quite the gift. Let's go open the store. Newt, you want to join us?" Steph asked.

"No thanks, but I will stop in later," he said with a wave as he headed out.

"Let's get some coffee."

"You and your coffee," Steph said shaking her head.

Steph was waiting for Sayer in the car. When Sayer came out Steph did a double take. Not only was Sayer sporting the dark eye makeup, but she was in all dark clothes and was carrying a box.

"Are you really going for the Goth look?" Steph asked her when she slip into the car.

"No, I just feel like changing my look."

"Well, alrighty!" Steph said backing out of the driveway.

"I think I have enough stock to open up shop," Sayer replied.

"Let's do this," Steph said.

Sayer was feeling very confident with her new powers. She walked into the coffee shop with a swing in her step. Nick looked up. At first, he smiled, but then if faltered. "Hi Nick. Can I have one of your wonderful coffees?"

"Sure, thing Blue eyes. You look different."

"Let's just say things are changing," Sayer said with a sly smile

"OK," he replied but his voice sounded unsure. He handed her the coffee. Sayer paid and was on her way out the door. Nick turned to Steph. "Is she okay?" he asked.

"I don't know. She is discovering herself. It is all a shock to the system. I hope it all settles in and she doesn't go all dark and stuff," Steph said as Nick handed her a coffee.

"Keep an eye on her and let me know if I can help, OK?" Nick said. He had a sad look on his face.

"Thank you. I will," Steph said.

Steph went next door and Anne greeted her at the door. "Hi. How are you? Sayer told me that you guys are going to open up the store!" Anne clapped her hands with a broad smile.

"Yes, we are. Sayer has a knack for this stuff. She has been working on all kinds of things with lots of success. I haven't had much luck but then, I haven't tried to do much stuff."

"Don't worry. It will come. Sayer is out back checking on the product I packed away when your grandmother's left," Anne said.

They got to work bringing everything out and setting up the shelves the way they felt they would look best. They put on some music; hung up the talismans; and set up crystals so they reflected the sunlight coming in the back window. Sayer found some scarfs in the back and hung them up and draped them giving the area a cozy feeling. Steph lit some jasmine incense intensifying the effects that Sayer started with the scarfs.

Sayer hung some black rocks next to the back door.

"What are those?" Steph asked.

"If I did them correctly they are to ward off ill doers. I found it that book and I gave it a shot. We will see what happens or doesn't happen," Sayer said.

“Is that what you were doing all morning?” Steph asked.

“Yes,” she replied.

Steph didn’t like the looks of them. They made a chill run up her spine. “I don’t know. Can something go wrong?”

“I don’t know. I don’t think so?”

“You do know that if nothing ever happens we will won’t know if they work. The only way we will know that they don’t work is if something happens,” Steph said.

“Let’s just hope we never find out if they do or do not work,” Sayer said “and stop being so logical. It takes the fun out,” Sayer said smiling.

Steph got a bad feeling about them but shook it off. She was being jealous and that was stupid. She knew she should be happy for Sayer and her talent.

The girls worked into the evening. Anne came in with sandwiches for everyone. “Thank god. I am starving,” Steph said, and she grabbed one off the plate.

“I have keys for you that way you can open up and close up when you want. I usually open the store around 10 but you can do whatever you want. We do have internet service in the store. The pass word is in the register drawer,” Anne told them.

“You have no idea how much easier you just made my life,” Steph said to Anne.

“How so?” she asked.

“Now I can bring my work here and manage a store at the same time! I am getting swamped with work from back home and it is going to cost an arm and a leg to get internet to the house,” Steph said.

“With a little rearranging we can get a desk in here and set you up,” Sayer said.

Anne walked to the front of the store with a smile on her face. It was feeling as it should once again.

Chapter 15

The next day Steph went poking around in the storage room. Sayer sipped her coffee and looked through the display case when she heard long scraping sounds. She looked up as Anne came walking back from some the front of the store. What is that noise?" She asked. Sayer shrugged. "It must be Steph out-back." The next thing they saw was Steph's butt coming out of the back room dragging a table on its side.

"Look what I found," Steph said as she turned around. Sayer snorted, and Anne started to giggle. "What?" Steph asked.

"You look like a real witch; you have cobwebs in your hair and dirt all over you. Were you lying on the floor?" Steph looked alarmed and brushed at her hair. "Get it off. Get it off. Get it off."

"OK. Okay, relax," Sayer said fluffing the rest out of her hair.

"I found this table. I can use it for my computer. A make shift desk," Steph said. She was pleased with herself. Sayer and Anne helped her drag it out the rest of the way and set it up. Steph found a folding chair too. She got to work making a spot for herself.

Anne was happy that the girls were there.

The three women got into a routine. They opened the store at 10, one of them would go next door for coffee (usually Sayer, so she could see and flirt with Nick.) and for the first half hour, they planned the day and had their coffee.

Business started off slow but as word got out, the business started to pick up for Steph and Sayer.

Working together was easy for everyone. Anne managed the store. The girls had a nice business going on in the back and Steph was able to do her telecommute work. It was turning into a very comfortable routine.

Most evening they would go down to the beach and work out of the book the house gave them about control. They had both mastered working with the water and the air. Now they were working on controlling fire. That one seemed to be a difficult for both.

One evening as they were practicing Steph said, "I think the problem is we are using the wrong kind of fire." She was poking her wand at the fire they had started in the fire pit. "What if you need to create the fire to control the fire?"

Sayer leaned pack on the picnic table." You may have something. Look it up in the book with that crest thingy on it and I will put out this fire. Then we can try again and make one on our own," Steph turned and pulled a funnel of water out the lake and put the fire out with it. She had a look of pride on her face.

"Well done but now everything is soaked," Sayer said. Steph winked at Sayer then whirled up the wind and aimed it at the fire pit instantly there was a big pile of smoke. Sayer thought that Steph had rekindled the fire with the wind but when the cloud settled she saw black figure standing next to the pit. She started cracking up. Steph was covered in black soot from head to toe. All you could see was two eyes blinking. "I guess that was not the best idea," Steph walked over to the lake to try and wash some off her face.

"Why don't you just make another funnel of water and aim it at yourself?" Sayer suggested still laughing.

"Very funny," Steph said standing there with the arm crossed.

Sayer walked over to the pit. "Hey at least the wood is dry."

"OK let's try this again. Is there anything in the book on how to make fire?"

Sayer started going through the book looking for instructions.

Steph pointed her wand at the pit and tried to imagine fire in the pit. She hoped it would just ignite.

Sayer looked at her. Steph's eyes were wide open, and the most serious expression on her face. "You look like you need to poop!"

Steph mouth started to curl up in the corners. She was trying as hard as she could not to laugh. Finally, she couldn't hold it in any longer and let out a muffled laugh and at the same time a new buff of smoke puffed out of the pit covering Steph in more soot. This stopped her laugh instantly. Sayer was beside herself cracking up. Steph just started up the hill with Sayer following behind cracking up. "We will figure this out. Hey, you know what tonight is?" Sayer yelled up to Steph. While catching her breathe from all the laughing.

"No" Steph said in a harrumph.

"It's the full moon," Sayer said.

Steph stopped walking up the hill turned to Sayer. "Really? I will take a quick shower and help you." Her bad mood had vanished.

Sayer went into the house and gathered up the ingredients she needed to make the medicine bags. She put them into a box and carried them down to the beach and set everything up on the picnic table. She started a small fire in the fire pit, once again with matches. Steph joined her mostly clean just a tidbit bit of soot left here and there.

"Feel better?" Sayer asked.

"Much better. Fire with matches?" Steph said.

"Yup" Sayer replied.

Together, with Sayer reading the recipe/instructions and Steph adding the ingredients to the caldron and chopping up the herbs, they had it ready in no time.

Sayer looked around. "We need to set this over the fire, bring it to a boil and leave it simmering in the moonlight until morning. How are we going to hold it over the fire all night?"

Steph walked around the yard looking for a stick, thinking they could wedge it between some rocks and have it hold the cauldron over the fire. Suddenly she saw something glimmer in setting sun. She walked over to a tree and found a metal rod leaning against it. She looked around the ground and found more metal pieces. She took them all back to the beach.

Sayer tried to balance the small caldron on a rock close to the fire. She noticed Sayer playing with metal rods. "What are you doing?" she asked her.

"I found these over by that tree," Steph said gesturing to an old willow tree. Sayer joined her; looking at each piece. Steph took two of the pieces back and said, "It looks like some sort of contraption. Let's see how all the parts fit together."

"This rod looks like a shepherd's hook," Sayer said holding one up. She held a long rod that was bent at one end, so it went in the opposite direction but then turned up again. The kind you hang plants in gardens, but it had ridges on the main part of the rod.

Steph had the other parts and had formed a base with a hole in the top. The Shepherd's hook fit in perfectly. Steph picked it up and took it to the fire pit. She put it in the base close to the fire. "Hand me the caldron please," Sayer handed it to her and Steph put it on the Shepherd's hook and swung it over the fire.

"Nice!" Sayer exclaimed." Now we don't have to hold it all night. I was thinking we need to get some sleeping bags and take turns all night."

The girls sat down at the picnic table and waited for it to come to a boil. The cats had come down to watch them and now all three were curled up next to the fire. The loons were making a ruckus in the distance. "This really is peaceful," Steph said.

"I love it," was all Sayer had to say.

Steph leaned her head onto Sayer's shoulder and they watched the fire.

Chapter 16

With a fresh coffee on the table, Sayer got busy assembling the medicine bags. She spread everything on the counter in the back of the store. They had opened the store at 10, but Anne was not in yet.

Steph was behind her, working on her computer. She had the journals from the house, ledgers, and all kinds of grafts spread out. She was trying to get work done from her job back in NH, but she kept getting sidetracked with figuring out their history.

The bell on the door started to chime. "Maybe it is Anne?" Sayer said as she got up and walked toward the front of the store.

Steph heard mumbling voices. She figured Sayer was correct. Sayer came back and said that it was George and he wanted to talk to them together, so she should come up and hear what he had to say. George is the town cop. Everyone knows and likes George. Not much crime happens so he walks around each day making the rounds. He gets free coffee at the Cup of Joe. When he stops by the sub shop up the street he gets free sandwiches. Sometimes you can drive by the town beach and catch him asleep in his cruiser. The most action he gets is breaking up parties that the high school kids have at the beach and an occasional speeding ticket. Not many arrests. Sometimes when someone is too intoxicated he will let them sleep it off in the cell. They always wake up with a pillow under their head and a blanket over them. The town jokes that it is a five-star jail cell. George is just an all-around nice guy.

Steph joined them at the front of the store as George said that someone had broken into Anne's house overnight.

"Oh my god! Is Anne okay?" Steph exclaimed.

"Don't know. I was hoping she was here," George replied.

"We haven't seen her. I was just about to drink her coffee for her," Sayer piped in. Steph just looked at her.

"Well, if you think of anything or see her please call me." George asked of the girls.

"Absolutely." The said in unison. George left them with his card with his cell phone number on it.

"I wonder what happened," Steph asked. "I hope she is okay." with a side-way glance at Sayer, Steph asked "What do you say that we lock up the store and go check out her place?"

"Don't you think we should leave that for the cops or cop?" Sayer asked her.

"No," Steph said as she turned the sign to "Closed," Sayer though that she really liked this side of Steph as she removed the apron she put on to protect her cloths.

They jumped into Steph's car and they headed out.

Anne lived about ten minutes away from the store. They pulled up to Ann's house which is an older New Englander style house. It was white but with bright red doors and shutters. The door had a strip of crime scene tape stuck to it. The girls pulled the car around back and got out. They walked around the house checking it out. The doors looked fine and there were no broken windows. The back door had crime scene tape across it too. Steph reached between the tapes and tried the doorknob. It was not locked, so she pushed the door open. She looked at Sayer, shrugged and climbed between the tapes and entered the house. Sayer followed her. "I thought you said we should leave it for the cops," Sayer asked her. "No! You said that! They are not here, and I love mysteries," Steph said.

"We are going to get into trouble," Sayer said but the glint in her eye said the she didn't care. "Are you sure you want to do this? You seem to be the 'follow the rules' kind of girl," Sayer asked.

"I just want to have a look around," Steph said innocently and batting her eyes. Sayer just smiled and followed her in.

The back door opened into the kitchen. All the cabinets and drawers were open and stuff was everywhere. To the right was a dining room which was virtually untouched. They walked towards the front of the house into the living room. This room, once again, was trashed. To the right was a hallway going to the kitchen from the front door and it had a stairway to the upstairs. The girls headed upstairs. All the stairs squeaked going up. "It would be hard to sneak in or out of this house. "Sayer said.

"Did you ever sneak out"? Steph asked her.

"Yup. I sure did," Sayer told her.

"I never did. I didn't have anywhere to sneak out to," Steph said.

The upstairs had a bathroom and three bedrooms. The bathroom was untouched, but all of the bedrooms had been ransacked. Someone was looking for something.

"I wish we knew Anne better and had seen this place before. Then we would notice if something was missing," Steph said. "But I did notice that she has some things hanging around the house that came from our department at the store. We should take them with us and see if we can figure out what they are for.," Steph walked over to one of the windows to get a better look and noticed something on the windowsill. "Sayer, look at this?" Sayer walked over, "It looks like sand. Why would she have sand on her windowsill?"

"Do you have your phone?" Sayer asked.

"Yes," Steph said.

"Take pictures of them that way we will not be disturbing the crime scene," Sayer suggested.

"What are you doing in here?" A deep voice said from behind them? They screamed, jumped, and swung around. Steph, just about fell over. George was standing there with a sub in his hand.

"This is a crime scene and you just violated it. I should arrest you," he said. There was fury in his eyes.

"I am so sorry, George, but we are worried about Anne and we thought we could help. We didn't touch anything. We promise," Steph said her voice sounding desperate. She was scared. Sayer had the feeling that Steph had never been in trouble with the cops. Sayer had Steph's phone and was taking pictures of something hanging in the window without a care in the world.

"What are you taking pictures of?" George asked her.

"I just like this thing hanging in the window. I am going to try and recreate it to sell in the store," Sayer lied.

"Why don't you girls just get out of her and leave this alone. If I find you in here again I will arrest you for tampering with evidence." George said to them. "OK," they said in unison and bolted out of the house to the car and drove back to the store.

"See what you did! We are new in town and you may have just put us on the cop's radar. I have never been on any cop's radar. I never even had a speeding ticket," Steph was exasperated.

"Did you hear George coming up the stairs?" Sayer asked her. "And it was your idea!"

"Obviously not! He scared the shit out of me," Steph said ignoring the part that it was her idea.

"Well, do you remember how loud the stairs were when we climbed them?" Sayer asked Steph while looking at her while she drove. "Yes," Steph said taking her eyes off the road and giving Sayer a quick glance.

"Why didn't we hear him?" Sayer asked.

"I don't know," Steph was pouting about George busting them and thinking about what she had observed at the same time.

"Don't sweat over it, the door was not locked so we just opened the door and went in. We didn't really do anything wrong. We didn't touch anything," Sayer said trying to reassure Steph. "Except cross crime scene tape. No big deal," Steph said.

The rest of the day at the store was the busiest ever. They were not selling anything but everyone in town had heard about Anne and was stopping by to see if they could get any details from the girls. They told them that they are as clueless and the rest of the town. They didn't tell anyone that they had been to the crime scene.

It did make the day go by fast.

Chapter 17

Two days passed with no news about Anne. They started to get worried. On the third day, Sayer was busy in the solarium. She had the tunes cranked to tune out the loud purring. She had three cats at her feet. She was repotting the catnip and they were very interested in what she was doing.

Steph was in the living room going through the original recipe book. The one Sayer used to make her potions and medicine bags. She was trying to figure out what those things hanging from her windows were. She decided to take a break and make dinner. She went into the kitchen. She took out some chicken and a bunch of vegetables. She opened the window between the kitchen and the solarium. "Sayer can you give me some oregano, basil, parsley and a garlic bulb," Steph asked. Sayer handed her the stuff and as Steph worked on dinner and Sayer worked on the plants, they tossed ideas off each other. Steph had all the veggies chopped up and in a bowl. She added some pepper and salt. She stopped and stared at the salt that had spilled on the counter. "I know what that stuff on the window sills was!"

"What window sills?" Sayer asked through the window.

"At Anne's, remember the sand? I was thinking she needed to do some spring cleaning, but it wasn't dirt it was salt!" She exclaimed. Her eyes were lit up.

"Why would she have salt on the window sills?" Sayer asked.

"I don't know. I did read once that you can use it to keep demons out. I wonder if she had it at the doors too. May be those things hangings were to keep demons out."

"Demons! Are you crazy? Demons are not real," Sayer said.

"Did you think that witches were real or just stories?" Steph asked.

"Touché," she replied.

"Where am I going to get info on demons? The internet would be full of information but how can I sort on what is fact and what is fiction," Steph was thinking out loud.

"Ouch." She yelled and spun around. Something had hit her in the back of the head. There was a book on the floor. She picked it up. Again, it was an old book. It was thick, and leather bound. Steph was rubbing her head. "I guess the house knows and for future reference, duck when you think out loud," Steph said to Sayer. Sayer laughed, enjoying the show.

"Thanks house, but next time, chime a bell or something. Give me a warning," Steph said to the air.

"I love this place," Sayer was smiling.

• • • • •

Over dinner they poured over the book that the house had given them, and the book that Sayer used to make the talisman. They were trying to see if they could make some kind of connection.

"Listen to this Steph," Sayer said as she read out loud. "There are different ways a person could summon a demon. Most ways are done intentionally but a few could happen by accident.

To summon a demon intentionally a person or persons need to follow a set of defined rituals. Usually the person or persons who do this feel that they will be able to gain from the demon but the usually end up doing the demons bidding.

A person could summon a demon by simply playing with a Ouija board at the wrong place. You could summon a demon by doing a ritual, or by an inexperienced person or persons just playing around. Sometimes, but very rarely, a demon can be attached to an item and an unsuspected person will come into possession of the object and then the demon can use this person to do its will."

"I think we need to go to Ann's for one more look," Steph said to Sayer.

"But I thought you didn't want to get into trouble," Sayer said standing up ready for another adventure.

"We are already on the radar. We just can't get caught this time. It will be quick. I just want to see if I am correct about the salt on the window sills. We should go tonight in the dark," Steph said.

"If you say so," Sayer was smiling.

Once the sun had set, the girls got ready. They put on dark clothes and black hooded sweatshirts and headed out. They pulled into the back of the house. Steph handed Sayer a flash light with a cloth over the end. Sayer looked at Steph with a questionable expression. "It is so it will not be as obvious that we are in the house with flashlights from the outside."

"Oh," Sayer said.

This time the back door was locked. Steph was disappointed. She was hoping it was still unlocked.

"Let me see," Sayer pulled out a bobby pin from her hair and got to work on the lock. In just a few minutes the lock clicked to the unlocked position.

Steph whispered to Sayer. "Do you always carry a bobby pin?"

"No, but I had a feeling. The door is always locked in the movies," Sayer said with a wink.

The girls crept into the dark house keeping the flash lights aimed at the floor hoping to not attract any attention to the house.

"Yup there is salt all over the house. Even by the doors on the floor and you can tell people have walked through it so, if a demon was here it looks like it was searching for something and Anne knew it," Sayer said.

"What could she have that a demon would want?" Steph asked while rubbing some of the salt between her fingers. The girls continued to look around.

"It cannot be too big because only the drawers are dumped out," Steph commented.

"Look at this Steph," Sayer said standing by a door in the kitchen. Steph walked over to her and saw what Sayer was pointing at. There were dark scuff marks on the floor going through the door. The lock on the door was busted. It was locked on the kitchen side and the way the wood was splintered, it seemed like something pushed its way out of the basement.

Sayer opened the door and the two of them made their way through the door. Once they were inside Sayer closed the door.

"What?" Steph exclaimed but then the lights went on.

"No real windows in the basement. This feels like a cheap horror movie. They never turn on the lights and I have always wondered why," Sayer said.

Steph just smiled at her cousin and they moved down the stairs. It looked like a normal unfinished basement. It was all concrete walls and floor. In one corner were a washer and a dryer and a shelf with the normal basement items of leftover paint, unused wall paper and boxes for old useless electronics that no one ever throws away. The walked around the bend to the back of the stairs and they both froze in place. Burned into the wall was a star with what looked like a face in it. It was a gruesome face. The chin was pointed, and it had long horns coming out of the top of the head. The girls turned and ran up the stairs.

"How the hell did George miss that?" Sayer yelled as they ran out of the house. They didn't even try and be quiet or relock the door.

Chapter 18

The girls went straight to the shop and went in the back door. Steph booted up her computer and started searching for any information they could find about the symbol. Sayer started to search the bookstore for any books that may help. Sayer came back with a stack of books. For the next few hours they searched. They found lots of information. So much, that they did not know what was true or not true.

"I think we need to call Newt!" Sayer said.

"It is late. Close to midnight. I don't want to wake him, and what are we going to say? Hey Newt! We broke into a crime scene and saw the devil," Steph stated.

"Basically, I think we should. He knows more about this stuff then we do. I am going to call him. As soon as the sun is coming up we are calling him. Deal?" Sayer asked.

"Deal. But in the meantime, I am going to keep digging while we wait," Steph told her.

"I am going to camp out on the coffee shop door step. I need some air" Sayer said as she headed out the door.

Sayer was back ten minutes later.

"You are back so soon? Did you pick their lock too?" Steph asked her.

"No, Nick lives upstairs and he saw me outside. I guess he was up and happened to look out the window and saw me sitting there. He made us two coffees," Sayer said as she handed Steph her coffee. "I filled him in on what we did, saw, and thought."

"What? You told him how we broke into a crime scene?" Steph asked he, shocked that Sayer had told him so much.

"Yes, and he was cool with it. I think he sees us as rebels now." The girls had a much-needed laugh.

"So, what did he think about it?" Steph asked.

"He said it makes him uncomfortable. I suggested that maybe Anne was a devil worshiper or something," Sayer told her. "He said absolutely not."

"He is ok with witchcraft?" Steph asked.

"Seems to be, but we are not very good witches yet. He also said he would like to help us but I said, 'no thank you'. We have no clue to what we are doing and if something goes badly I don't want anyone else to get hurt. Remember what I did to that oil lantern?" Sayer said.

"Good call," Steph agreed. "It is early enough, let's call Newt."

While Sayer was on the phone Steph kept looking through the books. Sayer came back." Newt is on his way. He said not to do anything more just sit here and have our coffee. We are young and inexperienced. We don't want to read something out loud and, with our powers, accidentally set something loose."

"Holly shit. Really? I didn't even think of that," Sayer said.

Thirty minutes later a tall woman came walking in the door. She locked the door behind her and checked that the sign still read closed. She found the girls in back. They were sitting there with huge eyes and were ghostly pale.

"It is going to be okay." She assured them in a deep voice. The two girls just looked at her until realization dawned on them.

"Thank god Steph called you!" Sayer had tears in her eyes. "I have been sitting here thinking about all the stuff we could have let loose. I am so scared. I don't want to be a witch anymore," Sayer was fully crying now. Steph put her arm around her and was crying too.

It took Newt thirty minutes and two more coffees to calm the girls down to hiccupping, snot running messes. "You girls have been up all night, had the scare of your life and you are emotionally drained. Go home and get some sleep."

"Don't you need us? I don't know if I can sleep," Steph said while sniffing and blowing her nose.

"You will not be too much good to me in this state. Go home, get some sleep and I will call you if I come up with anything." Newt instructed them.

"Okay, but why are you dressed up as a woman?" Sayer asked him while blowing her nose. Steph elbowed her in the ribs.

Laughing Newt said. "Oh, I forgot. I was just getting dressed for an early, dress rehearsal for next week's show. The only time we all have together is Saturday morning. I am playing one of the characters in Rocky Horror Picture show. Don't I just look fabulous?" he winked at the girls. That got a smile out of the girls and they agreed to go home. They showed Newt what they had learned so far and went home.

Once they were home they could not sleep. Sayer went to Steph's room and knocked on the door.

"Come in," Steph said.

She opened the door and Steph was sitting in bed, on her computer, looking stuff up. "I can't sleep," she said looking up to Sayer.

"I can't sleep either," Sayer walked over to Steph's bed and crawled in with her.

"OK," Steph put her computer away and lay back down on the bed. Sayer reached out and grabbed Steph's hand. "I am glad you are here. I will miss you when you leave." The girls fell asleep holding hands.

CHAPTER 19

They slept late into the next day. It was overcast with dark stormy clouds moving in. When Sayer woke up, she looked out the window at the clouds. "I have a bad feeling." She went down stairs and found Steph on the couch.

"Let's get back to the store. I want to swing into the police station and talk to George," Steph said.

"Do you think we should tell him what we found?" Sayer asked her.

"No. I don't want to piss him off. I just want to see if he has learned anything more that we can tell Newt."

They drove into town in silence. Each girl had huge bags under their eyes. They didn't even bother to change their cloths. They were a mess.

They stopped at the station and George was on the computer.

"Hey George, did you learn any more information?" Sayer asked

"Nope just what I told you at the store yesterday morning."

"We are sorry again that we went into the house," Steph said.

"What? When did you go into the house?" George looked up from his computer for just a moment. They noticed dark circle under his eyes. "I haven't been back to the house since the first initial investigation. I haven't seen you girls since I stopped by the store."

"That is what I mean, since we saw you at the store," Steph said quickly shooting Sayer a glance.

Sayer looked at her with huge questionable eyes. Steph gave mouth "quiet" to her. George was looking at his computer once again so he didn't see it.

"I am sorry girls, I would love to talk but I cannot talk about an investigation. It looks like I will have to call the FBI and get them involved. I hate to do it and have the feds crawling all over our town, but I am at a loss," George said with a heavy sigh.

"No worries. We will let you work," Steph grabbed Sayer's arm and pulled her out of the door.

"What was that all about?" Sayer asked.

"Thank god he is so stressed he didn't pick up on my blunder. Something is going on. You saw him yesterday at the house or am I losing my mind?" Steph asked Sayer.

"Nope. I was with you and I saw him," Sayer replied.

The girls stopped at the market and grabbed some sandwiches and chips. Everyone they saw inquired about the disappearance of Anne. It was what the whole town was buzzing about. When they got back to the store Newt had lots and lots of books stacked all around him.

"Did you find out anything?" Steph asked as she handed Newt a much-needed sandwich. He was still dressed as a woman, but his wig was next to him on the table and his mascara was smeared under his eyes.

"I have been looking through so much information it is beginning to mush together so I started to take notes. It is a demon; but what we need to figure out is which demon has her. It doesn't matter how it was done just that it was done. We need to find out what it wants from her or what it wants to trade for her. Demons are from a different dimension and somehow a porthole was opened up."

• • • • •

"You think a demon has taken Anne?" Steph asked. She was as white as a ghost.

"Definitely," Newt told her. "That is the only reason for that that symbol to be burned into a wall."

"They trade?" Sayer asked in shock.

"Oh, yes. They want all kinds of things. They steal too. I have known of lesser demons to trade for sparkly things. The type of things kids would have who get involved in with Ouija boards and things. Some demons like to play jokes like with séance's. They basically will just come through for the fun of it and play with the people's minds that are holding the séance. These are the simple ones. There is not much danger with them. Sometimes the bigger ones with come through but that does not happen very often. It takes a lot to get them through. The eviler a demon is the more magic is needed to get them through."

"Do you have any idea what we are dealing with?" Sayer asked"

"I have been trying to narrow it down. We need to gather more information, so we can figure out what to do. Do you remember anything else that may help? Is anything missing from the store?"

"No. Not that we can think of. But we haven't been here long," Steph said.

"You said that there was a picture on the wall in the basement of Ann's house. What I am trying to figure out is how and why it is there. I know for a fact, that Anne is not into black magic. She is a Wiccan but nothing else. She knows the danger of it."

"Do you know what to do to get rid of it once we figure out what it is and wants?" Sayer asked.

"No but I do know that it will take a lot of magic to send it back and close the port hole connecting the two dimensions. We need to go to the house and look at the sign and what is around it."

"Anne has all kinds of salt on the window sills and talismans hanging in the windows. It is like she was scared of something," Steph told Newt.

"Even more reason to go check it out." Newt said.

"George said that he was going to have to involve the FBI we should go quickly," Sayer said.

"Do you have your bobby pin?" Steph asked Sayer.

"Yes, I have it in my pocket," she said.

"What do you need a bobby pin for?" Newt asked the girls.

"To pick the lock with," Sayer said.

"You are a witch. Remember?" He reminded them.

"I didn't even think of that?" Steph said while she slapped herself on her forehead with the palm of her hand.

Chapter 20

"How are we going to keep from getting busted by George?" Newt asked. He was no longer dressed like a woman. He took a quick shower at Nick's and he was in jeans and a sweatshirt and looked as he should.

"I have an idea," Sayer looked in the mirror and re-did her ponytail. Then headed next door to the coffee shop. Steph turned to Newt. "That girl has a problem. How is coffee going to help?" Sayer came back in with Nick and a new guy. He was tall, dark, and handsome. And he was huge; the kind of guy you would see in Gold's Gym commercial or quarterback football player. Steph was dumbfounded.

"Newt, Steph this is Jake," Sayer said.

"Jake this is Newt and my cousin Steph," Sayer introduced the hunk of a man.

"Hi" was all Steph could get out she reached forward to shake his hand but somehow tripped over her own two feet and fell into his arms.

"Well I guess you are falling for me." Jake said helping Steph straighten up.

Steph turned bright red. "Sorry I am a klutz." He was the best-looking guy she has ever seen.

"My pleasure," he purred.

Steph turned to Sayer trying to get her composure. Trying to pat down her fly away hairs and then remembered she was still dressed in yesterday's clothes and probably had massive bed head. Sayer had turned around and you could see her shoulders shaking from laughter. This just made Steph get even redder. “What is going on Sayer?”

Sayer turned around, her hands were on her cheeks, tears were running down her face and she said with as much of a straight face as she could manage. “They are going to run interference. Nick is going to call George and tell him that Jake was caught stealing from the coffee shop and get him to come to the store. They are going to argue.” She stopped and took a few breaths to compose herself a bit more and continued “The idea is that they will keep George in the coffee shop while we do what we need to do. I will call Nick’s phone let it ring once when we are done and then he will drop the charges against Jake.” She was still giggling.

Jake looked at Steph “If I get arrested will you bail me out?” This just made Steph go red once again and she started to stutter. “Y—Yes.”

Nick came to her rescue.” Come on Romeo. Let’s get into a fight.” The boys walked out of the shop punching each other back and forth in the arms.

“I am so embarrassed,” Steph gowned.

“You’re not very good at flirting, are you? You need more practice,” Sayer said smiling at Steph.

“Come on girls, let’s go. We don’t have time for a teenage romance.” Newt said.

“What romance?” Steph said red once again.

They rode over to the house in Newts car. Every time Sayer looked at Steph she started to laugh again. Steph sat quietly in the back-seat pouting.

They pulled around the back of the house and went to the back door. Sayer looked to Newt. “Okay, how do we unlock the door?”

“I don’t know. You’re the witch.” Newt said.

Steph pushed her way past them and pulled out her wand. She circled the wand around the door knob while holding her other hand up toward the lock. Her eyes were closed and then they heard a soft click.

“How did you do that?” Sayer asked amazed.

“I don’t know. I just did it.” Still pouting, she crawled through the crime scene tape again and marched through the door. “I focused on the lock to get my mind off that show I just put on back at the store.”

“And a good one it was. You should do standup comedy,” Sayer said.

"Just shut up" Steph replied as they walked through the kitchen.

"It's this way Newt," she said as she led him down the basement stairway. They got to the bottom of the stairs and went around the back and there it was, just like it was before.

Newt walked up to it. Put hand up and touched it.

"What are you doing? Don't touch it," Steph exclaimed.

"It is not going to suck me in. I am trying to get a vibe from it."

Steph and Sayer looked at each other.

Newt turned around and walked across the room he reached up and pulled a piece of sheetrock blocking a window. It was a small basement window at ground level. He ran his hand on across the sill.

"What do you think?" Steph asked Newt.

He walked all around and looked at everything. "I have no idea but there is no salt on the sill and it looks like something was hanging here. Do you see the scuff marks on the window? Did you take one of whatever was here?"

"No! When we saw that thing on the wall we ran," Steph told him.

"OK. Let's go." Newt said.

On the way back, Sayer called Nick's phone and hung up after the first ring.

They went back to the store and to the pile of books and notes they had left out. A few minutes later Jake came knocking on the door. Sayer greeted him and led him to the back of the store.

Sayer was joking with him about his short life as a thief. Jake walked over to where Steph was standing. "How did it go? Did you get what you needed?" he asked her.

Steph dropped the book she was pretending to read, stooped down to pick it up and knocked her head on the counter. Jake reached down and helped her up. He tilted his head to the side and gently touched the spot where she hit it. Her breath caught in her throat. "Are you okay?"

"F Fine, thank you. It didn't hurt," Steph spit out. "Thank you for helping us."

"Anything for Auntie Ann."

"She is your aunt?" Steph asked, surprised.

He shrugged, "Yup it is a small town."

"What can you tell us about her?" Steph asked. Her nerves seemed to be calming down.

"Just what everyone knows, she loves books, history, this store, and your grandmothers," he said.

"Was she into anything weird?" Newt asked him.

"Like besides sharing a bookstore with two witches? No." Jake said smiling. He had a brilliant smile that made his eyes shine.

"I am going to go and look in her office again see if we missed anything," Sayer said.

"I will go into the storage room and see if I can find anything," Newt said as he walked into the storage room.

Steph suddenly found herself alone with Jake. She didn't know what to do with herself, so she started to tidy things up; or at least tried to look like she was. Jake watched her as Steph moved things around aimlessly. "I know you are new in town. How about we get dinner some time? I can show you the sights," he said to her.

"I don't think this is the time or the place. Your aunt is missing and you're asking me out?" Steph said exasperated. Steph looked up into his handsome face. She debated about changing her mind. He was so good looking. That smile was making her knees weak.

He took a step closer looking down at her. "Are you sure?"

"For crying out loud, yes!" Steph said, keeping her ground. Just because he is god's gift to women doesn't mean he can ask anyone out at any inappropriate time, she thought.

"Okay, then," he said as he turned around and walked out of the store. She couldn't help but admire his back side as he walked away. He was very broad in the shoulders and narrow at the hips.

"Dang, he is fine," Sayer said as she walked back in.

"He has a fat head and a huge ego. He can keep it to himself," Steph said

Sayer just smiled and called to Newt that it was all clear.

"You purposely left me with him?" Steph asked.

"Yes" Sayer said.

"No, I didn't," said Newt. "I wanted to look around. I am trying to find clues. I think I have narrowed it down to three types of demons."

"How did you do that?" Steph asked him still trying to tame her bed head.

"The process of elimination. We know it is not a female demon by the picture. That narrows it down. The first one is a Familiar. They can be a girl or a boy, but their main purpose is to assist in witchcraft. It's not doing that, so it is out.

The second one is an Incubus, but they are sex addicts and I don't see any evidence of that. It may be a poltergeist. The place was a mess but for some reason I don't think so.

The third one is a Jinn. A Jinn can take on the look of someone else, so it is hard to identify." New said reading off his notes.

"Wait! What?" Steph asked.

"A Jinn is it a demon that can look like someone else." He looked at her over his reading glasses that were perched at the end of his nose.

"I think we saw one," Sayer said.

"When?" Newt looked from one girl to the next. Sayer had paled and sat down.

Steph turned to Sayer and said, "Sayer, remember when we went to the house and George snuck up on us and told us to leave."

"Yes, and then when we saw him at the police station and we apologized again for breaking in, he acted like he didn't know what we were talking about," Sayer finished for Steph. "I bet that was a Jinn at the house, not George."

Newt sat down and put his elbows on his knees and his forehead in his hands.

"Well, now we need to find out how to get rid of it and get Ann back. Can we do a séance and summon him and ask for her back?" Sayer asked.

"That seems too easy, but we could try." Newt said.

"I know what to do," Steph said. She started to gather some things throughout the store. "How do you know what to do?" Sayer asked her while following her around the store.

Steph turned to her and said "I have read a lot of books, as you know, and when it comes to doing a séance they all seem to be basically the same. I think the best place to do it is back in Ann's basement."

"I don't want to go back there. It's creepy. Are you sure you know what to do?" Sayer asked.

"Yes, I think so, but I need more people. Three is not going to cut it," Steph informed her.

"I bet Jake will help you," Sayer said.

"Let's keep him out of it," Steph said.

"I will go talk to Nick," Sayer said as she turned and walked out of the store.

"He is going to get sick of talking to you and helping you out," Steph told her.

"No, he is not," Sayer said with wink and went next door.

Chapter 21

"Hey blue eyes. You need more coffee?" Nick said with one eyebrow raised. He was cleaning up for the day and had just turned the "OPEN" sign off.

"No. I have had enough. Thank you. But we need you and maybe a friend or two. We think that a Jinn has taken Anne and is keeping her for one reason or another. We want to do a séance and see if we can contact it and find out what it wants and how we are going to get her back. Don't ask Jake please. Steph seems annoyed with him."

"Too bad, He likes her. He is not used to being turned down." Nick said and then asked." What is a Jinn?"

"A demon and she thinks he has a big head," Sayer told him.

"Wow, a demon with a huge head. Interesting." Nick said.

"No! Jake has a big head," Sayer said smiling.

"Well he does, and it is driving him crazy that she is not falling at his feet. You know he is the classic popular boy in school and all." Nick said. "Played football, dated cheerleaders, had excellent grades all without trying. It drove me nuts all through high school, but I could not have asked for a better bud."

"I don't think he is her type anyway. I will get the details about the séance and let you know. OK?" Sayer asked him.

"Sure thing, blue eyes," Nick said with a wink.

• • • • •

Sayer walked back to the store. Steph had a box and was putting black candles in it." When are we going to do this?" she asked."

"Midnight tonight," Steph answered.

"Oh," Sayer said with surprise in her voice. "How many people do you need? Nick is in and he will get some friends."

"Call him and tell him as many as he can get. The more people who are together the more powerful we will be," Steph told her.

Sayer hung up her phone." He will meet us there.I told him that we do not have permission to do this, so he can't be seen going into the house."

Newt went home to get a quick nap. The girls continued in the store preparing for the séance.

At eleven that night, the three of them went back to the house and parked in back. The door was still unlocked. Steph thought that it is odd that George had not been back to do more investigating. The climbed between the crime scene tapes and used flashlights to guide them to the basement door. They switched on the light and continued down the stairs. Sayer was hoping that the thing on the wall was gone, but there it was, just as they had left it.

"You know, it is not so scary when you know it is going to be there." She looked at Steph. She had a container of salt and was pouring it on the floor. "What are you doing?" She asked her.

"We need to make a pentagram, but it has to be large enough for us to sit inside it. The salt will protect us from the spirit," Sayer and Newt watched her as she poured out the salt. The shape was forming but then Steph stopped. "I ran out of salt. Can one of you see if Anne has any in her kitchen?" Sayer ran up the stairs and searched the cabinets. She had just found some when there was a knock on the door. She turned around and there was Nick and three other people she did not know. "Hey blue eyes. Are we in time?" "Yes" Sayer said. "This is Marge, Makala, and Suzie. Marge and Makala work for me and Suzie is their friend." Nick introduced everyone as they all climbed through the crime scene tape. "HI." "HI." "HI." Came from all the girls. Then Makala said. "This is so exciting. I have never done this before."

"Don't get too excited because we haven't either and have no clue what we are doing but thank you for your help" Sayer said. Marge turned to Susie and whispered, "I don't think this is a good idea." Suzie replied. "If you want to go, go, but I am staying."

Together the group made their way down the stairs. When they circled around the stairs, Marge let out a scream.

"I know. Pretty shocking isn't it," Sayer said stepping in behind them. Steph looked up with an annoyed look on her face. Sayer handed over the salt and repeated the introductions. Steph finished making the pentagram on the floor. Then Steph turned to the group and said "Thank you for coming. Everyone take a seat inside the circle, and hold hands," Steph walked around and lit all the candles and everyone sat down. Steph, then Newt, next to him sat Sayer then Nick, Marge, Makayla, and Suzie. They all clasped hands.

"Now remember, no matter what happens do not break the circle. I do not want to scare you, but I have never done this before. I am just going with the stuff I found in the journals left by the witches before us and the stuff I have read in books," Steph started to chant in old English, demanding the Jinn to come forward from his own dimension and speak with them. She repeated her commands over and over again. The temperature dropped, and a breeze picked up slowly going in a circle around the group and then started to pick up speed. It became so cold that each person could see their breath. Sayer looked around. Each one was looking at each other with terrified expressions except one girl, Makala, who had a look of excitement. Steph had her eyes closed and started chanting louder. The candlelight flickered and made odd shadows in the room. The drawing on the wall began to glow, and the smell of rotten eggs penetrated the air. Sayer shook Steph's hand to get her attention. Without missing a beat in her chants; she looked up at the wall across from her. The face in the center of the pentagram started to change. The face came stretching out of the pentagram all the way across the circle. "What makes you think you have the right to summon me little witch?" the face asked. It was even more disturbing than before. The skin was a greenish gray, the horns were black at the ends like dried blood. The teeth were all pointed like spikes. Its tongue was long and split like a snake. Steph was as pale as a ghost with her heart in her throat and her eyes wide staring at the Jinn. She was frozen in fear.

"I do!" Sayer said louder than she intended and looked around quickly.

The Jinn turned and looked at her.

"Another witch. Who are you? What do you want?" He asked of Sayer.

"I want Ann back," Sayer stated. She was hoping she sounded more confident than she was. She thought she made just have peed a little.

The gruesome face started to laugh. All the features became even more distorted. "Well too bad. She is mine." The face started to retract into the wall.

"We can trade for her." Newt said quickly. The face stopped and came forward to Newt's face." Why would I want to trade with you?"

"Then why did you take her if you don't want to trade her for something?" Newt asked the entity. His voice was shaking.

The Gin got real close to Newt's face. His breath smelled of rotten flesh. "You know I could fry all off you now."

"No, you can't! You cannot hurt anyone in the circle," Sayer blurted out.

The Gin looked down at the salt. "You think a line of salt could stop me?"

"Yes," Steph said with all the confidence she could come up with.

The gin looked at her for a few seconds. "There is something I would trade for her although I am getting used to having her with me."

"What do you want?" Steph asked with a shake in her voice.

"I want the crystal that I was trapped in, so no one can trap me in it again." The gin screamed spraying everyone with his fowl spittle.

"How are we going to find that? What happened to it when you came out?"

Screaming, "I don't know. Get it or Ann stays with me."

He flew backward into the wall and all the candles went out. There was a scream and Steph turned on a flash light. Newt walked to the wall and flipped on the light switch. Suzie was crying. Makala was open mouthed. Nick was looking back and forth from Steph to Sayer and Marge was quiet.

"Well, I guess we know what he wants and what it searched the house for," Sayer was walking around the basement thinking out loud. "It must have been a crystal hanging in the window and when the moonlight shone through it, it burned the pentagram on the wall letting the Jinn out. Now we need to find that crystal, trade Ann for it and re-trap the Gin." Suzie got up and left without a word. Marge followed Suzie. Makala said "I am going to go with them, but thanks. That was freaking scary." She got up and left. "I guess I will go too. I drove them," Nick told Sayer with a shrug.

Sayer walked over to Nick and gave him a hug. "Thank you for your help."

"I may regret saying this but anything for you, blue eyes," Sayer smiled at him "Thank Makala, Marge, and Suzie for us.

"I will." And Nick left.

Newt started to pick up the candles. "Steph, why don't you grab the broom and brush away the salt. Let's get out of here." Together they cleared away the evidence that they had been there and headed to the house.

Chapter 22

They were successful of getting back to the house without seeing George. The three were exhausted and collapsed into the chairs in the living room. The cats all curled up with them. Newt preferred Charlie in this lap. He claimed that he claws on the lynx paws make him nervous.

"So how do you think we will be able to get Ann back?" Sayer asked Steph and Newt while absentmindedly petting the cat.

"We have to find what he wants and give it to him unless you have a better plan," Steph said.

"What do you think happened to the crystal?" Sayer asked.

Steph got up and left the room. They could hear her moving around in the library. Steph came back with a few journals in her hands." I don't know, but I figure we should look through the journals and see if we can find any clues." She handed one to Newt and one to Sayer. Sayer wrinkled up her nose. "This is going to take forever."

"If you have any better ideas let's hear them," Steph said. Sayer just opened the journal and began to skim the pages. There was nothing to be heard except the turning of the pages. After a while Sayer got up and made everyone tea. Then she went back to the journals. They spent the next few hours going through journal after journal. Steph kept getting up, putting some back and getting more. Everyone once in a while someone would say "Hey I got...never mind." and went back to reading.

As the sun was coming up Steph got up to make coffee. Newt dozed on the couch. Sayer was on her sixth journal when she said, "Steph I think I found something."

Steph came running from the kitchen. "What?"

"Look at this." there was a drawing of a black crystal and under it was written (Jinn, keep in a closed space not accessible to the light of the full moon) and under it is a spell that would get the Jinn into the crystal. "The journal is dated back to 1845. I think it is the same one," Steph read out loud to Sayer. "It looks like our ancestors may have had to deal with him before." The girls were excited and started to shake Newt who was snoring. He was slow to wake up. Finally, they had a cup of coffee in front of him and he began to understand what they were saying.

"OK, we know what the crystal looks like, and we know the spell to use to get him into the crystal, and how to keep him there. But how are going to get to him to put himself in the crystal?" Sayer said.

"Well at least we have a start. Let's find the crystal and then we can figure out what to do next. Too bad we don't have a way to get his dimension and talk to Ann" Sayer said. "Too bad we can't go down a rabbit hole," Steph replied.

"Do we have to use the same crystal? Can we use a different one and just shove him back in there?" Sayer asked.

"I don't think it is that simple. If it was, he would have asked for all the crystals." Newt said. "Let me see that picture again?" Steph handed the page to him. "This is so old. Have you found any stuff like this around the house while you have been here?"

"No," Sayer stood up and said "Hey house? Do you have crystals hidden in you?" She ducked her head with her arms over it. "You never know," she said peeping up. Newt was looking at her. "The last time I was thinking out loud for something the house shot it at me and hit me in the head," she informed him.

"Oh," Newt said chuckling. Steph with her hand still protecting her head walked around the house with Sayer looking to see if anything had shown up on any tables and cabinets. No luck. "That would have been too easy," Sayer said.

"Agreed, but worth a shot," Steph said putting her hands down.

Newt got his stuff together and headed home for the night or, actually, the rest of the morning. Depending how you looked at it. It had been a long forty-eight hours. Sayer and Steph let the cats out and locked up the house. Steph noticed that the cats once again jumped up onto the roof when they left. She thought that there must be something up there that they liked. She wished they had found a way up. Sayer took Charlie and headed up to bed. Steph looked out back and admired the view of the sun reflecting off the lake, then headed up too.

Chapter 23

Mid-afternoon the next day, Steph got out of bed and headed down stairs but was blinded by streams of colors everywhere. It was like she was walking into a rainbow. She yelled up the stairs "Sayer you want to see this," Sayer came halfway down the stairs and stopped. "Oh my god," she exclaimed. The entire house had crystals hanging everywhere. They were hanging from the ceiling, the cabinets; they were even hanging in the fireplaces. It was throughout the entire first floor. "I guess the house had a few," Steph said. "Thank you, Majka. You outdid yourself."

"Majka?" Sayer asked.

"It's a name I came up with for the house. It means mother in Bosnian."

"Oh, fancy. I like it. I think it fits her. How did you come up with it?" Sayer said.

'It just came to me. I don't even know any Bosnian. It was in a dream I had last night. I just looked it up" Steph said.

"That is freaky," Sayer said taking a step away from Steph.

"Hey," Steph said pouting.

"I don't want you to start having dreams about me," Sayer said.

"Don't worry I never remember my dreams; except last night's," Steph said.

"Let me know if you dream of me growing a sixth toe or something," Sayer asked.

"Okay," Steph said giggling. "I will let you know when you get a third eye."

They took the crystals down and placed them carefully into a box.

As they handled the crystals; they looked at each one carefully to see if one resembled the one in the picture. They were all shapes and sizes. Some were long and skinny and some were short and fat.

After they had them all gathered, they spread them out and examined them each not knowing what they were looking for but still looking. "I don't know how we are going to do this? Can we put a spell on a lot of them and use them all and hope that one sucks him in?" Sayer asked.

"That is exactly what we are going to do. I don't see any other way. We are so beyond our experience," Steph said. Sayer looked at her with fear in her eyes. "It is the only thing I can think of. Do you have any idea what to do?"

"No" Sayer said, defeated. She walked over to the box of crystals and took some back out and started to hang them up.

"Why are you doing that?" Steph asked.

"If we are going to attempted this we need all the positive energy we can gather. These will help. I am going to make each of us medicine bags to wear and I will charge a few of the crystals with moon light. Plus, I also like how they make the house look hanging all over the place."

When she was done hanging the crystals in the windows, she got to work on the medicine bags. She pulled out the old tattered book and looked up the strongest most powerful stuff she could find. She knew she was going to need all the help she could find. After a few hours she looked out to the lake and saw Steph pointing her wand time and time again at the fire pit, as she looked down at the book in her left hand. Sayer decided it was time both of them took a break and walked down to the beach.

Chapter 24

"What are you doing?" she asked.

"I am trying to make white fire. It can hold the demon while we get Ann. It is very difficult to do. I don't know if I will be able to do it," Steph told her.

"Let me have the book. I will read you the instructions," Sayer suggested.

Steph handed the book over. Sayer read to her, step by step. They tried different ways of saying the words of the spell; thinking that maybe they were saying it incorrectly. They started to take turns tying the spell. They knew that they would need it. After a few hours, they decided that they needed a change of scenery, so they decided to head to the store.

They parked the car behind the store and went in through the back door. All was quiet. There were a few messages on the answering machine for some book orders. Steph walked to the front of the store. She did not switch the sign to open. It was late in the day, but she did notice something on the stoop outside of the door. She walked back into the store carrying a basket of flowers. "What is that?" Sayers asked.

"Flowers," Steph said.

"No kidding, Captain Obvious. Who are they from?" Sayer asked.

"I don't know but my name is on the card," Steph said. She put them down on the table. Sayer walked over and sniffed the flowers. "They smell wonderful. Read the card. I am dying to know who your admirer is" She said smiling at Steph.

Steph opened the card and read it. Laughing she read the card out loud. "My heart longs for you, my soul cries for you, my eyes burn for you, my empty arms reach out for you." They are from Jake. Can you believe it? Does he really think that is going to work?

"It is kind of sweet, stupid, but sweet. It doesn't even rhyme," Sayer said.

"No, it is just a play for him," Steph said as she crumbled up the card and tossed it into the trash.

"Nick says he really likes you," Sayer told her.

"He just wants to make a notch on his belt. I am not going to degrade myself like that," Steph said.

"What if he is sincere?" Sayer asked.

"Time will tell. If he is really interested, he is going to show me without all the glitter and muscle."

"You also need to learn how to walk and talk around him. You cannot fool me. I know you think he is cute," Sayer informed Steph.

"Damn right he is, but does he have a brain? Does he think on his own? Does he have any values? What is he made of? There is more to a man than looks.' Steph said.

"OK, OK," Sayer said putting her arm and giving up the argument. She thought Steph's got it bad and doesn't want to admit it.

The bell chimed for the door and Nick walked in, a cup of coffee in each hand. "Hey. I have been keeping an eye out, looking for you."

"Hi Nick." They said together.

"Any news, what's going on?" Nick asked as he handed them coffees.

Are you trying to get us hooked on these?" Steph asked?

"I think it is too late for that," Sayer said sitting down to enjoy her coffee.

"It will keep me in business. I am trying to get the town hooked on it. That is my big plan," he said and winked at Sayer. "What about that Demon thing?"

"Sayer, why don't you fill Nick in and I am going out back to poke around see if I can find something useful," Steph went into the back-storage room and started going through boxes being careful not to break anything. Steph found more boxes of crystals but none looked like the one in the journal but made a mental note of where they were. She came across an old wooden box and when she opened it an old rotten dried up foot of some sort fell out. She let out a cry of surprise but quickly recovered. She carefully used an old rag to pick it up and put it back in the box. She found some music boxes and wondered why they would even have them. She came across a mirror that must have been warped because when she held it up to look into it, the reflection was all wavy and her image didn't stay in focus. She put it on the pile of stuff she was collecting to bring into the store. She thought it would be fun for the kids in the children's section of the store. After a while she gathered her treasures and went back into the store. Sayer was all alone at the counter. "Did Nick leave?"

"Yes, he had to get back to the shop. He said he will help if he can when it is time," Sayer told her.

"You guys are getting close," Steph mentioned.

"He is a nice guy. We have a lot in common," Sayer said.

"Like what?" Steph asked.

"We both like me," Sayer said, smiling and batting her eyes. Steph gave her a playful smack. "I hope he knows that you are interested in him."

"Oh, he knows," Sayer said with a sparkle in her eye. "What did you dig up?" she asked.

"Check this out! I found it out back. Look into it," Steph held up the mirror and Sayer stepped in front of it. Her reflection went in and out of focus." Isn't it cool?" Steph asked. "I thought we could hang it in the children's section. It would be fun for them," Steph leaned it against the wall until she could get some mounting brackets. Sayer went back to what she was doing, and Steph cleaned up the music boxes to put out on display. Sayer kept walking over to the mirror and staring into it.

"What are you doing?" Steph asked.

"There is something about this mirror. I just can't get it," Sayer said.

"It is just an old mirror," Steph said.

"I know," Sayer said and walked away. Steph walked over to it, looked into it making faces at herself. She was feeling goofy and walked away.

The door chimed, and a woman came in with a few kids, so Steph went to assist with the customers. Nick must have left the door unlocked. Sayer found some mounting brackets and set to work making a space to hang the mirror.

She hung it up and gave it a good cleaning. More customers came in, so she went to help them. They only had an hour left so they left the store open and the rest of the day went by quickly.

Once the customers had left Steph said, “Let’s go home.” They locked up the store and headed back out. Jake was leaning against Steph’s car. “Hi,” he said.

Steph looked up into his eyes and her knees almost gave out, wondering why this guy did this to her. She regained her composure. “Thank you for the flowers.” She was hoping he couldn’t tell how nervous he was making her. Her stomach was all jumpy.

“I forgot something inside,” Sayer said and disappeared to give Jake and Steph some privacy.

“It is my pleasure. I was hoping to take you to dinner.” Jake said.

“No thank you. I have stuff to do,” Steph said.

“I can help you do stuff.” He offered.

“I’ve got it covered thank you,” she replied.

“I just want to get to know you,” he said to her. He did look sincere, but Steph didn’t trust him.

“I am trying to help your aunt, so please back off. I am not interested,” Steph said.

He stepped towards her and took her hand. Steph felt light headed. “It means a lot that you are doing all of this for her and I just want to show my gratitude.” His voice was like smooth chocolate.

“You can show me when she is back,” Steph tried pulling her hand back.

“I am going to take that as a promise,” he said with a wink.

“Fine, do that.” Steph could not believe she just agreed. What has she gotten herself into? Her stomach was all over the place. Jake kissed the back of her hand and walked away.

Steph fell into her car and put her head against the steering wheel.

The passenger side door flew open and Sayer flopped into the car. “So, what did Mr. Glamorous want?”

“He wants me to go to dinner with him,” Steph told her.

“Did you say yes?” Sayer asked. She was bubbling with excitement.

“I said I would once Ann is back,” Steph sighed.

"Excellent. You need a life," Sayer told her.

"Hey! You don't have one," Steph said sitting up in the car.

Sayer wiggling her eyebrows said, "Who says I don't."

"I know. You have Nick," Steph said.

"Not yet but I will. Let's go home," Sayer suggested.

Steph started the car and home they went.

Chapter 25

They were up with the sun the following day and opened the store on time. It was very busy for a Saturday. Steph worked mostly in the bookstore for Anne, and Sayer handled their booth. She sold her talismans for protection. The word had gotten out that Anne was missing so everyone was taking all the protection they could get. No one knew what happened to Anne, but they seemed to know it was something not normal, since Anne was a Wiccan and shared a store with two witches. Sayer tried to find out more about the Wiccan religion thinking that there may be something that could help them. Out of nowhere they heard a scream coming from the children's department. Sayer dropped what she was doing and ran. There was a small girl screaming next to the mirror that they had hung up.

"What is going on? What happened?" Sayer asked.

The girl was in her mother's arms. "I saw a face in the mirror," she was crying.

"Oh yes this mirror is one of those funny ones that make your face look different. It is ok sweetie," Sayer was saying to the child trying to comfort her. The girl looked up into her mother's face.

"There was a face with my face." She told her. Her mother hugged her and looked at Sayer over her shoulder. Maybe someone was standing behind her. Steph had joined them. She went looking through the store. It could have been any of the patrons in the store. The mother and the child left the store without making a purchase.

"That is weird. I wonder what spooked her," Sayer asked.

"I bet it was her imagination," Steph replied

"I am sure it was," Sayer said taking a second look at the mirror.

Newt came strolling in. "Hey girls." He had a suit and top hat on.

"Hi Newt. Another show?" Steph asked.

"No. I just like this costume. It reminds me of the good old days. I found some interesting information that I think is going to be useful." He had some papers in his hands.

"We have lots of crystals. Majka had a stockpile," Sayer said.

"Majka?" Newt asked.

"It is the name we gave the house," Sayer said, like people name their houses all the time. "I will grab them, I left them out back." referring to the crystals.

Newt looked at the mirror. "This reminds me of something. I just can't get it. Oh well, it will come to me. Anyway, I contacted one of my friends down in New Orleans. He has heard about this type of thing before. He said that we need to form a spiritual circle and draw the demon out. But first we need to enchant the crystal we plan on trapping it in. Unfortunately, demons can smell enchantments, so we need to fool him and once he comes out, and the crystal is presented, he will be sucked in. The tricky part is going to be getting Ann back before we put him in the crystal. He has to be in our dimension while we get her out of his."

"That is a lot to happen in a short time. We need a detailed plan and the enchantment," Steph said.

"I got the enchantment. My friend in New Orleans is voodoo priest and he gave it to me." Newt said.

"Okay, let's do some enchanting, shall we?" Sayer asked. Steph flipped the sign to closed and they went out back. As Sayer walked past the mirror she saw something flicker. She figured that there was something wrong with the mirror, it gave her the creeps, so she took it down and brought it out back with her.

As they spread out all the crystals, Newt pulled out a list from his pocket and they started to read off what was needed. The girls gathered all the stuff from around the store.

"We need one more thing. A dead monkey's hand," Steph said.

"What? Where are we going to get one of those?" Sayer asked.

"We have one. Hold on," Steph went out back to the storage room. Sayer just looked at Newt with a confused expression on her face. Steph was back in a minute with an old metal box. "I just found this when I was going through things. I thought it was disgusting so I left it where I found it. I didn't realize what it was until you said a monkey's hand."

They chose four crystals. Then they got to work mixing things together. The mix was purple and as it bubbled, it smelled like dead fish. Newt gagged, and Sayer turned green. Finally, they lowered the crystals into the brew using the monkey's hand. Then they pulled out the coated crystals and covered them to exclude any light.

"I think we should put them in different boxes and take them out one at a time," Sayer said. She grabbed some of the jewelry boxes they used for the crystals they sold. One by one they enchanted the four crystals. When they were done they flushed the rest of the brew down the toilet and opened the windows to air the place out.

Sayer was walked past the mirror and stopped dead in her tracks. "It is Ann! Look in the mirror!" she yelled. Newt and Steph came running. They were all stared at the mirror and sure enough Anne's face would come and go. It was like looking through fog. She was pale and had dark circles under her eyes and was mouthing something.

"What is it Anne? Are you okay? What is she saying?" Steph was asking. "Anne, we cannot hear you." If she would stay focused, we might be able to tell what she is saying. "Anne can you hear us? Can you get closer?" Sayer was yelling at the mirror.

Her blurry face came closer.

"I think she is saying help me." Newt said.

"We will Anne. We will. We are trying to figure out how," Sayer yelled to her.

Anne just kept mouthing, "Help me."

Sayer had the feeling that Anne could not see them. She had to walk away.

"I think time is of the essence here." Newt said as he turned to the girls. "Do you have a plan? She doesn't look too good."

Steph had a vacant look to her. "She looks like crap. Okay," she said. She shook her head and with determination she said "We need as many people as we can get. I have been looking through everything I can find. I think the best way for us to do this is to gather as many spiritual people we can find. We cannot have one person who has doubts about what we are doing. We will have to form a power circle. We will have to have all the crystals ready and one person with each crystal ready to bring it out at the proper time, so we can trap the Jinn in it. That is why we are going to have four crystals. We know the Jinn is smart, so we will have to be smarter. We will have the protection of the medicine bags and the circle of Faith and we will have to perform the ritual at the witching hour."

"When is the witching hour?" Sayer asked.

"Three A.M." Steph said.

Sayer looked disappointed. "Why the long face?" Newt asked her.

"I like to be sleeping at 3 A.M.," Sayer said.

"You can sleep or help Anne, but we don't have time for such petty stuff," Steph said to Sayer.

"I was just trying to lighten the mood. I am sorry," Sayer was red in the face with embarrassment.

"Sorry for snapping. I know you are a wise ass. This is just stressing me out," Steph said.

Newt clapped his hands together. "Okay, now, tell me how I can help, and let's do this. Do you think we have enough time to get everything together, so we can do it tonight?"

"We already prepared the crystals and placed them in some jewelry boxes. So that is done. Sayer knows the ritual and she is better at all the magic than I am; so, all we have to do is get some people over to the house by two A.M.," Steph said.

"I will call Nick and see who he can get on short notice," Sayer said trying to be helpful to make up for her comment.

Steph placed the items in a box and Newt helped her. Sayer talked on the phone as she paced around the store. Newt covered the mirror with a blanket. "Why did you do that?" Sayer asked, ended her call. "If we can see Anne then who is to say something can't see us?"

"Good call Newt," Steph said closing the box. "Why don't you meet up with us back at our place?"

"Okay, see you there." He replied.

Chapter 26

When the girls got home, Sayer headed upstairs and sorted through the boxes of their grandmother's belongings. When she found what she was looking for she took the clothes down stairs and handed a cloak to Steph. "What is this?" She asked. "Remember we packed them up? They belonged to our grandmothers. It can't hurt to wear them tonight. Maybe they left some magic on them. They changed and then Steph went into the kitchen to make them something to eat while Sayer continued to review what they were going to attempt to do.

Sayer and Steph sat down to eat. Sayer had put three bowls of milk out for the cats who were purring at their feet. Steph was comforted by the calm sound the three of them made.

"You do understand just how dangerous this is?" Sayer asked.

"Oh, trust me, I remember that nasty thing coming out of the wall. One of us could die if not everyone is willing to help us," Steph said.

"I know," Sayer said.

The two lynx cats were looking back and forth as if they were following the conversation.

Sayer reached down and scratched Andromeda between the ears. She looked down at the cat and could have sworn she just saw the two lynx cats wink at each other. She shook her head thinking that it was just her nerves, and her mind was just playing tricks on her when Cassiopeia stood up on her hind legs and put one paw on Steph lap, so they were eye to eye and said. "We can help you," Steph and Sayer both jumped up onto the table knocking all the dishes over. "What the," Sayer yelled, and Steph yelled "Holy cow! They talk."

"Oh, the faces you made. It was priceless." Andromeda was laughing.

"Andromeda, you are not helping. They need our help," Cassiopeia said to Andromeda. "This is serious."

"Okay, fine! Give me a moment to burn that into my memory." The cat was chuckling.

"It is ok" said Cassiopeia "We are your familiars. We have been helping the O'Brian witches for generations."

"You are demons?" asked Sayer.

"NO! We are "familiars,'" said Cassiopeia.

"Wait" Sayer said as she climbed down from the table. "Newt told us about familiars. Does he know about you?" Charlie had jumped up on the table and was enjoying the feast of spilled food. Sayer put him back on the floor. He jumped up again. She shrugged. She really did not care at this point.

"No, he just thinks we are wild cats that have been around for a very long time. This is the form we chose when we became familiars," Andromeda said.

"When you became familiars? You can choose to be a familiar?" Steph asked still standing on the table.

"Yes, we chose to be Lynx cats. It was a compromise. I wanted us to become black house cats and Andromeda wanted to become lions. We battled over it for a while and compromise on lynx cats, but that doesn't matter now. We are not albino we are just old." Cassiopeia told them. She continued "We were the first O'Brian witches in this house and when we died we chose to become familiars rather then move on, so we could help with the future witches of the family."

"Why are you telling us this now?" Sayer asked.

"It is time that you know. We always wait until the witches of the time are trying to do something beyond their abilities. If they don't need us we don't reveal ourselves. We stay exotic pets. We try not to interfere if we don't have to, but capturing a demon is difficult and dangerous," Andromeda said.

"Especially with the hard time he gave us when we first sealed him in the crystal," Andromeda said.

"You have done this before? So, how can you help us?" Steph asked.

"We still have power, a lot of power and the knowledge gathered in 100-plus years. We will go with you and use our energy to help you," Cassiopeia told her.

"What about the other people around us? Will they know what you are doing?" Sayer asked her.

"No one will know what we are up to, but we will keep you safe." Andromeda said and under her breath "as best as we can; that is."

"Thank god," Sayer said as she sat down once again putting her face down in her hands. Sayer looked up and asked, "Can you teach us all we need to know?"

"No. You will figure it out and we will assist you when we feel you need our help," Cassiopeia said.

"What about Charlie? Is he a familiar too?" Sayer asked the cat.

"No, he is just a sweet cat. Fun to hunt with," Cassiopeia said. There was a knock on the door. The cats turned around and started to walk out. Charlie stopped what he was doing and followed them.

"Wait, I thought you were going to help us?" Steph yelled after them.

"We will be there when you need us. It is better that people don't see us." One of the cats looked at the door behind them and it flew shut.

Chapter 27

Steph walked to the door as she said over her shoulder. “Every day it is something new.” She opened the door to Nick, Makyla, and Suzie, two of the girls who came to the séance. “No one else?” Steph asked.

“No. There was no way Marge will ever come near you again. I did tell Jake. Sorry, but I thought the more the better. He said he would see what he could do,” Nick said.

“Okay,” Steph said with a sigh, thinking she would have liked to have no extra stress with the man of muscle hanging around. Her stomach was already full of butterflies. “Come on in make yourself comfortable,” she said inviting them in. As she was closing the door it stopped. She looked around and Newt had put his foot in the door. “I bought a couple of friends. “This Brian and Alisson. They are friends of mine from the theater. They want to help.”

“Thank you,” Steph said.

Alisson looked at Steph. “I am going to be in production of the Exorcism. I figure this will help me prepare for the character I am playing,” she said as she swept into the room with a dramatic flair. She had short brown hair cut in a bob. She was petite and dressed like she just walked out of a high-end New York boutique. She swept around the room looking at everything. Is this magical?” She asked picking up a long glass bowl. “No,” Steph said.

“How about this?” she asked looking at a long silver piece of metal.

"No that is an envelope opener," Sayer said giving Steph an amused look. Newt and Brian were just watching and smiling. Brian was around six feet tall. Clean cut and very tidy. He also had brown hair and bright sparkling blue eyes.

"How about this?" she asked peeking into a box. She shrieked and jumped back.

"Yes, that it is, if it is a dead monkey's hand," Sayer was happy to say. Newt was laughing. Brian was doubled over laughing so hard.

"Gross" she said, pulling a bottle of Purcell out of her purse. She didn't pick up anything else. She wrapped her scarf snuggled around her like it was some sort of protective shield and went back to Brian side. He looked at her and she mouthed "Just shut up."

Steph grabbed the box of the material she had gathered together. "Why don't we all go down to the beach? It is getting late and I want to go over everything." Everyone followed her out and down to the beach and gathered around the fire pit. Sayer put the mirror in the middle. Steph took out the four boxes and place one in the north, one in the south, one in the east and the last one in the west. To the small group of people, she said, "Everyone hold hands and let see how big we can make this circle." It was a discouragingly small circle. Steph wanted to have herself, Sayer, all the boxes and the mirror in the circle with them. It was tight. She looked around trying to come up with a way to make the circle bigger. "Would everyone take a step back and make the circle bigger without letting go of each other's hand. They all took a step back. It helped; but not by much.

"Did we miss anything?" Someone yelled from up from beside the house. They could not see who it was because the new arrivals were in the shadow of the house. Women started to walk down the hill. Steph looked at Sayer. "Do you know what is going on?" she asked.

"Nope," Sayer said.

At least fifteen women walked down the hill introducing themselves. The last person coming down the hill was not a woman but a big bulky guy. "Jake! Who are all these women?" Steph asked.

"My aunt's coven who else?" he said.

"You got all these people to come?" Steph asked.

"Yes. They are all my aunts' friends. They know how dangerous this is. They are not magical but the love they have and feel, will help with the circle," Steph had tears in her eyes. She walked over to him and gave him a hug. "I don't know what to say."

"Don't say anything but tomorrow we are going on a date." He leaned down and kissed Steph on the cheek. "You can do this." He whispered in her ear and joined the now very large circle. Steph looked at Sayer whose smile was going from ear to ear and her hands were on her heart. Steph mouthed. "Shut up." and smirked at her.

With the circle complete and the time coming up on three A.M., Steph said to the group. "Thank you everyone for coming. With this much energy and love we have created a powerful circle. We promise to keep you all safe, if we can. This is new to us and if you do not want to be here we have no problem if you leave. I do not know what is going to happen or if any of you are at risk." No one moved so she took that as a sign that they were all ok with it. "Okay, then," she said.

Steph and Sayer stood facing each other. Together they started reciting the words the Newt had provided. "With these words, we call upon the wind, water and fire. We call upon the great mother earth to protect us from the evil that has taken place, to pull Ann from the depths of her torment. To return her to us." The mirror started to shimmer. Ann's face came to the surface. She had tears running down her face with a silent scream.

Storm clouds started to move in. Lightning began to flash through the sky and struck the water. The smell of sulfur was thick in the air. Ann's face disappeared and was replaced with the gruesome face of the Jinn. He started to come out of the mirror. "Nice trick but you are not getting her," Sayer and Steph joined hands and continued with the chant. The Jinn came further out of the circle. Steph waited for him to be completely out. He was growing larger and larger but the end of him stayed in the mirror. "Don't think I will come out all the way witch. I am not stupid. Do you have what I want?"

"Yes, it is in the box at my feet. Come and get it." The Gin came further out. He was almost all the way out and Steph kicked back and knocked the cover off the first box. The Jinn saw her and made the crystal blow up. "I don't think so. You are young and unprepared to take on the likes of me."

You could read horror in the faces that made up the group, but they did not break the circle. They began to chant "With the sun, wind and the moon we protect you." They repeated the chant over and over again. They all closed their eyes either out of fear or because they didn't want to witness what was about to happen. No one noticed when two large cats joined the inside the circle. The sat next to each side of the girls facing out as a sign of protection. The Gin started to laugh. "You think you can do this? I will kill the four of you.."

Steph looked at him. Her face was blank, but her eyes began to glow an electric blue "Oh, I don't think so," she said with a calm voice almost a whisper. The eyes of both girls glowed brighter and brighter. The light from their eyes formed a mist and settled like a fog on the ground. The eyes of the cats began to glow just like the girls.

"We are going to take you and put you back to where you came from," Sayer said with a smile. The energy that the girls created caused the wind to blow and air cracked and leaves began to circle around the group going faster and faster. Their hair flew all around them. With their glowing eyes, they looked possessed. "Go ahead and try," Sayer said smiling to the Jinn as he came completely out of the mirror. He was huge. The cats started to circle around between the girls and the outer circle of women, making a protective circle between the two circles. Then Steph and Sayer let go of each other's hands. There were whispers in the group of the circle. Someone said, "Don't let go of each other's hands." The group started to chant once again slowly getting louder and louder. Steph went for the next crystal box, but the Jinn blew it out of her hand. "Don't think I am stupid enough to let you do that?" The Gin said in a deep voice that made the ground rumble and another crack of thunder and lightning rolled overhead.

"I do think you are that stupid and I am going to do it," Steph said and put her wand high in the air, brought it down in a circular motion and created a ring of white magic fire that encircled the Jinn. The Jinn desperately tried to get out of the circle of fire, but he kept getting blocked. He wanted to get back to the mirror. Sayer looked at Steph with complete awe and then she walked over to the mirror. She stepped inside the mirror and disappeared. Steph almost stopped what she was doing. Where had Sayer gone?

Chapter 28

As Sayer stepped into the mirror everything went black and she felt herself falling; then pain as she landed on her back, knocking the wind out of her. Her heart was pounding. Once she had her breath back, she started to feel around her. It was pitch black. The ground was cold and smooth, but she could feel a few pits as she ran her hands around her. She guessed it was rock. She knelt back on her heals and felt the air around her trying to see if she could feel anything Nothing was in her reach. She went down on her hands and knees and she put one hand in front of her, so she could feel if she came in contact with anything and started to crawl slowly forward. Inch by inch, she moved at snail's pace, stopping every few inches to reach out and feel the ground in front of her. She had no idea if she was going to crawl into a wall, an animal or just crawl over a ledge. Her eyes started to adjust to the dark, she thought she could see something in the distance on the ground. What had she gotten herself into? "Anne is that you?" she whispered so quietly she could barely hear herself. She slowly made her way to the lump. She reached out and touched it. It screamed so loudly that she screamed too. Her heart was pounding again. The lump sat up and pushed itself further away screaming. Sayer stopped screaming. It sounded like Anne. "Anne it's me Sayer. Anne, stop screaming so I can talk to you." Ann was flaring her arms all around her. "Anne, Anne stop. I am Sayer!" she screamed at her because talking to her calmly was not getting through. Anne stopped screaming instantly. In a cracked voice "Sayer? Is it really you?"

"Yes, Anne it is me. I came to get you out."

"Oh, thank the mother earth. You scared the bejesus out of me. How are we going to get out?" Anne asked.

"I have no idea?" Sayer told her. She was in what looked like a cave. A very deep cave.

"Do you have your wand?" Anne asked.

"Yes," Sayer answered.

"Can't you use that?" Anne asked.

"I have no idea. I haven't done much with it yet. I am still learning. Do you know how to use it? Sayer asked Anne.

"No, I don't," she said sadly. Sayer mover over next to Anne and sat close to her. "It is so cold," she said to Anne.

"I am freezing. I have been so cold for so long. I wish we at least had a fire to keep us warm," Anne said.

"Wait, I have been trying to make fire," Sayer stood up, walked some distance away from Anne, closed her eyes and with a circular motion brought her wand down and nothing happened.

Anne had started to quietly weep. Sayer looked at her and with fierce determination swung her wand up in the air and down one more time and fire appeared at the end of her wand. "Darn it. It's on fire" Sayer exclaimed. Swinging it around in the air.

Sayer, wait! Bring it over here. Sayer slowly walked over to Ann with her wand aflame. "Put it down here." Ann had a few twigs and some debris pushed together. Sayer put the flame on the debris and it caught. She pulled her wand away and the flame tip went out. Her wand was fine. Anne warmed her hands over the small flame. "This feels so good. Oh, my heavens."

In the flame light Sayer got a good look at Anne. She looked small and frail. She had dark patches under her eyes she looked like she had lost a few pounds. "Are you ok Anne?" She asked walking over to her and wrapping her arm around her to help warm her up.

"Now that you are here. I am much better," she said leaning into Sayer. "How are we going to get out?" Anne asked.

"I don't know," Sayer said again but just then a large cat simmered into view and slowly it became whole. "Cassiopeia, What? How? You just appeared. How? I don't understand," Sayer stuttered. "I am very old, and I know magic that you do not, you are young. With time, you may be able to travel between dimensions. If you become a strong enough witch. I doubt it though. It is very strong magic." the large cat said. Anne hid behind Sayer holding on to her to her back. Sayer could feel Anne shaking. "Sayer, you need to get me out of here. I am hallucinating that a very large cat is talking to you." Anne whispered into her ear. Then she felt the pressure of Anne leave her. Sayer swung around, and Ann was on the ground, unconscious. Sayer dropped to the ground. "Anne are you okay? Talk to me."

"Oh, don't worry about her." The cat said. "She just passed out. It is better this way. Now, I can get you both out of here and she will just think it was a dream," Cassiopeia said.

• • • • •

"Are you sure?" Sayer asked.

"Yes. Now let's get you out of here," Cassiopeia said.

"Whatever you say let's just go. What do I need to do?" Sayer asked.

"Just walk up the stairs," Cassiopeia said.

"UM what stairs?" Sayer looked around, squinting in the dark, looking for anything that looked like stairs."

"These stairs." the cat said and took a step up and was now floating six inches off the ground. Then she took one more step up and was once again, floating six more inches off the ground.

"I cannot see the stairs," Sayer said to the cat.

"Trust me. Trust in magic. Just because you cannot see it, doesn't mean it is not real," Cassiopeia said. Sayer turned around to get Anne but found her floating in the air behind her. Sayer was shocked. She blinked her eyes a few times to be sure she was not imagining it and turned back towards the cat that was now six feet in the air and climbing. Sayer took a small step forward until her foot hit something hard that she couldn't see, and she stepped up. Then she inched her foot forward until it another edge and she stepped up again. Anne followed her, floating through the air. They continued this way for a few minutes until Sayer looked down and got dizzy. She almost fell and had to crouch down. It was unsettling to find herself floating in the air with nothing under her. She thought she may just get sick. Cassiopeia turned around and said. "Keep climbing we have a long way to go."

"I have to get myself together. Give me a minute" Sayer said taking some deep breaths. "Can't you just zap us out of here?" Sayer asked.

"No, I cannot just zap us out of here. Keep climbing. Sometimes there are no shortcuts. You have to do things the hard way." the cat replied in a gruff tone as she kept climbing. "But you just appeared. Can you do that again?" "No." was the only answer Sayer got. Slowly Sayer got up and continued to climb. She didn't want the cat to leave her behind. She got to a point that when she put her foot out, she couldn't put it down. "Wait," she yelled to the cat. "I can go on, it's like there is a wall." The cat turned around." There is. It is a vortex. It is a separation point between dimensions. You must push your way through. What we are doing goes against the laws of physics. That is why you are hitting a wall." "Oh, okay," Sayer said. She pushed and felt it give a tad bit. She was afraid of pushing too hard and falling. She pushed a little harder and she felt like she was being squished as she moved forward. She felt the air move around her and push in on her. It was hard and tight. She continued to push and slowly she felt herself come out the other side. She pushed a bit harder and felt the front side of herself clear the end of the vortex. As she slowly pulled herself though, she could feel herself being sucked back. She pulled hard and fell forward on to the next invisible step. Her stomach dropped, she had a feeling she was going to fall off the invisible stairs. She turned around and noticed that she had only moved through maybe an inch of space, but it had felt like she had fought through four feet. She watched as Anne glided seamlessly along behind her. "Hey. How did Anne get through with such ease?" Sayer yelled forward to the cat, but she didn't get a reply. They climbed for a long time. Sayer got out of breath and her legs were shaking. She had lost count of how many vortexes she had to push herself thorough. She was exhausted, sweating and out of breath when the cat turned and said, "We are here." Sayer looked around and found herself hundreds of feet in the air and she had to squat down again or she was going to fall. The cat said "See that shimmer? Pull yourself and the girl through, and you will be back to the beach."

"Thank you," Sayer said, but the cat was gone.

• • • • •

Sayer came back out of the mirror pulling Anne out. She had her arms wrapped around her back and under her armpits. Ann's head was forward with her chin on her chest. She was still unconscious. She dragged her to the center of the circle and laid her on the ground. The Jinn screamed "NOOOOOOOO. She is mine."

"No, she not, you son of a bitch!" Jake opened a box and the Gin yelled as he was sucked into the crystal hidden in the box. Jake wasn't part of the coven circle, so he had been standing back and being quiet. But when Sayer and Anne appeared out of the mirror, he had snuck in and grabbed one of the two last jewelry boxes. The last thing they saw was his screaming face of the Jinn being distorted as it was sucked in until all that remained was a crystal filled with black whirling smoke Steph took the box from Jake and closed it and put a couple of rubber bands around it and handed it to Sayer. Sayer took her wand and magically sealed the box. The white fire went out. Everyone started to cheer. Then they heard some explosions and looked up to the house. Fireworks were launching out of the chimneys. Steph and Steph joined hands and laughed. The clouds cleared, and all the stars came out. "Wow" was all any of them could say and watched the show.

Chapter 29

Sorry I was gone so long," Sayer said to Steph. I am surprised you are all still standing here." "What do you mean?" Steph asked. "You were only gone a minute if that." "Really? It felt like I was in there for hours. I started a fire and had to climb a million steps," Sayer said. She was shaking all over. She had to sit down on the ground.

Jake walked up to Steph put his arm around her and said, "I will pick you up at 7 tomorrow night."

"I am looking forward to it," she replied in a whisper.

Sayer smiled up at her cousin. She noticed Cassiopeia watching from the edge of the dark woods. The cat nodded her head and headed back into the woods.

The coven had taken over caring for Anne. As she woke up she said, "You have to believe me. There was a huge talking cat." She tried to tell anyone who would listen about the talking cat, but no one believed her. They all thought she was just exhausted and her mind was playing tricks on her. With what she had just gone through no one was surprised. One of her coven mates was a doctor and gave her a quick exam. She was dehydrated and needed some food and lots of rest, but she should be just fine. Everyone milled around talking excitedly.

"Please everyone! Thank you so much for all your help. Without you, I don't think we could have done it. I would like to move Anne into the house and get some hot tea into her so please join us in the house," Steph said to the group.

The coven must have had complete confidence they would succeed, because they came fully stocked for a celebratory party. They pulled-out casseroles, breads, salad, soda, and lots of wine. Everyone drank ate and celebrated until day break.

George came by to check on the return of Ann. Steph had called him to let him know. "Listen George, there is a talking cat in the woods," she tried to tell him. "Okay, Anne I will keep an eye out for it," he answered her chuckling. "I think I need to get a few of these women home first though." He was very happy to be able to cancel the need for the FBI. He didn't want them in his town. A few of the women had had a tad bit too much to drink and George was more than happy to give them rides home.

The girls invited Anne to stay the night with them. She was happy to accept the invitation. She was not ready to be alone again. Anne made her way up to one of the spare rooms and fell asleep in the blink of an eye.

Steph and Sayer stayed up and started to clean up, when they heard a loud long scraping sound coming from the front entry. They looked at each other and ran to the front of the house.

The back cabinet that they were unable to open was wide open. It was not a cabinet but an elevator. Sayer said, "I know how we get to the third floor now."

"You think?" Steph replied.

"Who is the wise ass now?" She said, and they walked into the elevator together. The door closed. They hit the up button and the elevator started going up. They were so excited. They had no idea what they were going to find. At the top the elevator opened into a room filled with early morning sunshine. They were in the back of the room. Dried herbs hang from the ceiling. There was a long old wooden table that was covered with an assortment of items. It had knives; small bowls some beakers and cauldrons. The ceiling had large round skylight window. It was etched with a pattern of diamonds throughout. Facing the lake were two French doors that stood wide open to a narrow porch. There were two rocking chairs just inside the doors and it looked like there were two people sitting in the chairs. "Hello?" Sayer called out and looked at Steph. She was scared. She reached out and grabbed Stephs hand. They started to walk around the rocking chairs and gasped at what they saw. They were looking at the bones of their grandmothers. "We have found them," Steph said.

"Yes, you did.' a voice said. The girls spun around, and the cats came through the French doors. "You knew they were here?" Steph asked.

"Yes," Andromeda answered.

"Why didn't you tell us?" Sayer asked.

"Why should we have? They are fine. No one bothered them as they passed on to the next life," Cassiopeia said.

Steph shook her head, rolled her eyes she said, "We should call George."

"Let him sleep. It not like anything is going to change," Sayer said.

"Look Sayer, they died holding hands," Steph pointed out. Sayer looked at Steph she had tears running down her face. The cats each curled up next to a rocking chair.

"I am going to quit my job," Steph said.

"What? Really? What changed your mind?" Sayer was asking while hugging Steph.

"This place is way too much fun. I couldn't imagine it being any other way. Plus I have a date with Mr. Mussels."

Sayer was laughing and crying." Maybe we can double date some time."

"With you and Nick?" Steph asked.

"No, me and George, He kissed me goodnight tonight and what a kiss that was," Sayer said smiling.

"George did?" Steph asked smiling. "Ewe, no, Nick," Sayer said laughing.

Steph looped her arm with Sayers and said. "Let's get some sleep."

Chapter 30

In the morning Ann joined them for tea and muffins. "So, Anne what is the story? How did you end up with the Jinn?" Sayer asked Ann around mouth full of muffin. Ann put down her tea cup and said, "When your grandmothers disappeared I got spooked. I missed them terribly and I thought maybe something sinister has happened, so I went and did what I knew to do to keep away any evil. I gathered a bunch of the crystals and hung them in my windows and put salt down at all the entrances of my house. I will pay you for the crystals." "We don't care about the money, Keep them," Steph said. "But how did you get the crystal that the Jinn was in?" She asked. "That is the part I don't really understand?" Steph asked. "When your grandmothers didn't show up at the store and I could not reach them I went and woke George up from one of his afternoon naps at the beach. He was snoring away in his cruiser. When I told him I was worried about them, we came to the house together. The door was unlocked. They never locked it and we looked around. I found this old antique box, and inside was one of the most beautiful crystals I had ever seen. It was dark gray, and it looked like there was smoke swirling around in it. I put it up to the sun light to see if it would reflect any color and it did not, so I put it back where I found it. That is the last I remember about the thing. George continued with the investigation of their disappearance, and I went back to taking care of the store." Anne took a sip of her tea. Steph was looking at Ann and her forehead was wrinkled in concentration. She said, "How did it get out of the box and into your basement?" "I don't know." Ann said. Steph got up and went into the library and got the old journal where they found the information about the Jinn and the Crystal. She opened it up to where they left off when they were looking for information to the next page "It says here, that the crystal needs to be kept in a dark concealed box because gazing upon the crystal with the swirling smoke can cause a person to become compelled to take the crystal from the box without even knowing it. Well, that explains that. This time it has been magically sealed, but I think I will put a note on it saying 'Do not open. Evil inside.' just to be safe.: Steph said.

• • • • •

Later that morning they went into town to the police department to fill out the paperwork that George needed done. Anne was home for much needed rest and they decided to keep the store closed for a few days. No one would blame them. The girls stopped into the store and put a sign up saying they would be close for a long weekend but would re-open on the following Monday. Sayer walked into the coffee shop. Nick looked up and had a huge smile on his face. Sayer had dropped all the dark makeup and clothes. "Are you back to your old style?"

Sayer said "Yes. I don't like the dark stuff. Let it stay in the movies."

"I am glad Blue eyes." Nick had come around the counter and pulled Sayer into a hug and whispered in her ear, "This is the way I like you." and gave her a kiss on the cheek. Sayer turn three shades of red. He let her go and she stuttered, "Ca-Can I get a coffee?" Nick walked back around the counter, pleased with himself that he got her off guard. He saw a tad bit of the gentle girl inside the tough talking witch. Steph came in and grabbed a coffee with her. "Blue eyes do you have plans tonight?" Nick asked Sayer.

"Not after I get Cinderella ready for her prince," Sayer said, and Steph kicked her. "It is just a date and probably will be the first and last one."

Sayer looped her arm with Steph and said, "let's go get ready for your' just a date' night." Nick shook his head and waved goodbye as they left. Sayer stopped and popped her head back in the door. "Swing buy after you're done for the day." and she left.

Chapter 31

Steph and Sayer spent quite a bit of time picking out an outfit for Steph. Sayer was pulling out all of her "come hither" clothes and Steph had pulled out all her business suits.

"Steph, you are going on a date, not a business meeting," Sayer said to her.

"It is all I have. I went to business meeting, not dates," she said frowning at the micro dress Sayer was holding up for her to see.

"Okay, let's see if we can put something together."

Steph ended up wearing a short black skirt from one of her suits, a fitted blouse from Sayers closet that was too low cut for her liking, so they put a scarf around her neck. Steph pulled on a pair of black stocking and Sayer pulled out a pair of her black heeled boots. The looked they ended up with was softly sexy. "This I can do," Steph said to Sayer looking in the mirror with Sayer was standing next to her. "We do a good job together don't we?" Sayer said. "We sure do," Steph gave her cousin a hug just as the doorbell rang.

"Oh, do you want me to go down stairs and have Jake stand at the bottom of the stairs and you can make a grand entrance?" Sayer was saying just about bolting to the door.

"No, with my luck I will fall down the stairs because he is in the room," Steph said laughing "I will answer the door."

• • • • •

The bell rang a second time as Steph was just opening the door. Jake took a step back. “Wow, you look fantastic,” Steph turned pink and almost tripped out the door. Mumbling to herself “stupid heals.” Jake took her hand and led her to the car. He did not trust her not to fall again. “Where are we going?” Steph asked him. “It is a surprise.” He replied. They drove into town and parked in the back of the library. Jake opened the car door for Steph, put his hand out and helped her out of the car. He kept her hand as they walked to the back door of the library. “Our date is at the library?” Steph asked. “You don’t need to show me the library to impress me,” she said. “It is not the library I want to show you.” Jake said as he pulled out a set of keys and unlocked the back door. Steph had all kinds of butterflies doing gymnastics in her stomach. “You have a key to the library?” Steph asked skeptically. He replied with a simple “Yup.” He opened the door and let her in. He led her to the elevator and took her to the top floor. When the door opened they stepped into a large storage room. It was a square room with huge windows at each side and in each window was telescope. Jake guided Steph to the first one adjusted the telescope to Steph’s height and told her to look. Steph leaned forward and look through the telescope and she was in awe to see what she was seeing. The sky had blown up with stars. “Now you are looking at the Gemini constellation. If you come to this one over here.” Jake took her hand and guided her to the next window. “You will be looking at the Orion constellation,” Steph looked at him with amazement. He looked down at her, took her chin in his hand and guided her head back to the telescope. She was thoroughly surprised. She was still looking through the telescope when she heard the elevator open and wheels squeaking. She turned around and saw Nick rolling a table in and behind him was Sayer with a couple of bags. “What are you doing here?” Steph asked them. In an annoyed voice Sayer said. “Don’t look at us, we are invisible. Nick is making me help him. This is my date. Serving you. He said I owed him,” Steph giggled, and Jake led her to the next window that was facing the south.

With this one you will be looking at Hercules. Steph was speechless. Not only had she discovered a different side of Jake that she was really liked but she is seeing the galaxies up front like never before. He guided her to the last telescope. "This is the last one and my favorite one to look through. It is of Venus," Steph was enjoying her private tutor of the sky, but she could smell the food and her stomach started to growl.

Jake led her to the table that Nick and Sayer had set up. Jake pulled out a folding chair for her and then sat down opposite her. Nick opened a bottle of red wine and poured them each a glass while Sayer served them sugar cured steak with baked potatoes and green beans with bacon out of take-out boxes from the local high-end restaurant. Once Nick and Sayer were done serving them, they left. "How did you arrange all of this and how do you have this room all set up?" Steph asked him. "This is where I go to get away. I used to come to the library all the time and take out astronomy books. The librarian, who is also the owner, noticed. He showed me this room. He had an old telescope, which was once his son's, in a window and told me I could use this room whenever I want." He told her.

"I spent that entire summer up here. Once I got a job I started to buy better telescopes and eventually the owner gave me a key and said as long as I don't bring anyone here and always lock up I can use it whenever I want to. This drove Nick crazy. He could never find me but one day he followed me here and I was busted. I told him if he ever told anyone I would kill him. I guess he took my threat to heart because he never told anyone." "Why didn't you want anyone to know?" she asked. "This is mine and I don't want to share it." "But you are sharing it with me now. Why?" Steph asked. "Because you are the first person I have ever met that I want to share this with. Not only are you beautiful but you are smart. Not some girly frilly dumb girl," he said. "I am honored," Steph said blushing three shades of red.

They finished their meal, cleaned up the mess and headed to the car. Jake opened the car door for Steph. He stopped her as she stepped past him to get in the car. He put a hand on her back and with the other on he pulled her chin up and met her lips with his. The world stopped for Steph and her knees got week. He pulled away and said "Sorry. I had to do that while I still have the nerve," Steph causally whispered. "That's okay," as she fell into the car. She didn't think she would be able to walk ever again and he drove her home.

Chapter 32

Two days later with the help of Jake and Nick they had a small ceremony with the coven and buried their grandmothers on the hill next to the house. They planted a Apple Tree tree to mark the spot rather than a tombstone.

Steph and Sayer rented a truck and planned a road trip to get all of Steph's belongings. Charlie was running around with the Lynx cats pretending to be one of them.

The End

Keep an eye out for the next adventure for
Steph and Sayer